Citizen Suárez

Citizen Suárez

Guillermo Verdecchia

Talonbooks
1998

Copyright © 1998 Guillermo Verdecchia
Published with the assistance of the Canada Council.

Talonbooks
#104—3100 Production Way
Burnaby, British Columbia, Canada V5A 4R4

Typeset in Garamond and printed and bound in Canada by Hignell Printing.

First Printing: August 1998

Talonbooks are distributed in Canada by General Distribution Services, 325 Humber College Blvd., Toronto, Ontario, Canada M9W 7C3; Tel.:(416) 213-1919; Fax:(416) 213-1917.

Talonbooks are distributed in the U.S.A. by General Distribution Services Inc.,
85 Rock River Drive, Suite 202, Buffalo, New York, U.S.A. 14207-2170; Tel.:1-800-805-1083; Fax:1-800-481-6207.

No part of this book, covered by the copyright hereon, may be reproduced or used in any form or by any means—graphic, electronic or mechanical—without prior permission of the publisher, except for excerpts in a review. Any request for photocopying of any part of this book shall be directed in writing to Cancopy (Canadian Copyright Licensing Agency), 6 Adelaide Street East, Suite 900, Toronto, Ontario, Canada M5C 1H6; Tel.:(416) 868-1620; Fax:(416) 868-1621.

Canadian Cataloguing in Publication Data
Verdecchia, Guillermo.
  Citizen Suárez

  ISBN 0-88922-391-2

  I. Title.
  PS8593.E67C57 1998   C813'.54   C98-910717-5
  PR9199.3.V45C57 1998

For Tamsin

My schizophrenias are what I am, the active process itself. There is no medication to cure me....

—Rafael Campo

Earlier versions of "Letter From Tucuman" and "Money In The Bank" were published in *grain* (Autumn '95 and Winter '97); a version of "Surveillance" appeared in *Geist* (Spring '98); "The Necktie Revolution" first appeared in *Event* (Summer '97), and "A Day in the Life of Thomas Macomber" was first published in *Prism* (Spring '98).

Many thanks are due to Greg Hobson, Mara Coward, Camyar Chaichian, and Rosemary and Graham Kelsey for innumerable kindnesses: days on the island; excellent meals, conversation, correspondence, and child care, as well as material and editorial assistance.

Contents

The Necktie Revolution	11
A Day In The Life Of Thomas Macomber	23
Surveillance, or The Uncle's Disappearance	34
The Several Lives Of Citizen Suárez	36
Letter From Tucuman	77
Money In The Bank	83
Meteorite	96
The Dream Of The Library	108
Winter Comes To The Edge Of The World	118
Peace In Ixturria	130

The Necktie Revolution

The day La Señora died, a month long period of grieving was legislated. Special masses were held; schools, stores, restaurants, and movie houses closed. Radio stations were asked to play only sacred music, preferably requiems. They, naturally, complied with the official request. Television stations agreed to broadcast special programs about La Señora's life for an entire week. Flags were lowered; children did not play; car horns, normally so vociferous, took a collective vow of silence; dogs did not bark; no one sang; even *futbol* matches were cancelled. Lamentation and keening, ashen faces, wringing of hands were the order of the day, of the month.

The schools and cinemas closed only for a week and, of course, essential services such as the police did not reduce their efforts but went about performing their essential duties dressed in special black uniforms and looking sadder than normal.

Among the working and the rural poor, there were many who felt that their one chance for happiness had been extinguished forever when La Señora died. They would have mourned her passing without the legislative encouragement. She had given them a voice, as well as holidays, toilets, and weekends in hotels. She had been their instrument, their strength, their apotheosis. Every day, except Sunday, she sat in her office across from the Presidential Palace and heard their petitions.

"Señora, my husband has no work."

"Señora, my daughter is ill and we can't afford the medicine."

"Señora, I have never been to the cinema."

"Señora, I came only to see you, to bask in your light."

La Señora gave them whatever they needed, whatever they asked for: work, medicine, passes to the cinema, a kiss.... She worked unceasingly, tirelessly, often not even stopping to eat. She drew strength and sustenance from her people, or so she said. She worked until early in the morning, often retiring later than El Presidente himself. She wore out secretaries, administrators and assistants.

Some whispered that La Señora's work was nothing more than bread and circuses. It was also whispered that La Señora was of humble origin, the daughter of a cabaret dancer and a nameless father. The nation's oligarchy certainly subscribed to that story. The wives of the banana barons and the tin barons and the cattle barons despised La Señora because her Program For the Realignment of Social Conditions had usurped their traditional charity functions. The wives of the various barons claimed La Señora was uncouth, that she spoke poorly and did not know which fork to use at dinners. Some went so far as to say that her father was an *Indio* and that she was, therefore, *mestiza*, of mixed blood, a mongrel. The banana, tin and cattle barons admired La Señora's cleavage and warned their wives not to give offence, for La Señora's favour went a long way to securing the patronage and support of El Presidente.

But now La Señora was gone, and although many felt not a shred of remorse or loss at her passing, no one dared express such a sentiment outside the most intimate, trusted circles. Everywhere, from the most downtrodden, dusty villages to the most opulent, irrigated neighbourhoods of the capital, the outward show was of sorrow. The entire country wore black. No one smiled in public.

Oscar was a serious young man, a student of engineering who hoped one day to run a large corporation. A large, efficient, North American corporation. He was average-looking, of medium height, broad-chested and already balding (because he was too serious, his friends said). Oscar was, by all accounts and all reports, a moderate, reasonable, dispassionate young man. His older sister, Marta, said he had a Teutonic personality, which Oscar took as a compliment of the highest order. But for all his calmness, his equanimity and his rationality, Oscar had come to loathe La Señora and her husband, El Presidente. When he heard of La Señora's death, he was, inwardly, delighted, insofar as it is possible for a reasonable, moderate, Teutonic personality to feel a sentiment as extreme as delight.

Years ago, when El Presidente (who, at that time, was not yet El Presidente, only El Coronel) and his starlet wife first appeared on the national political stage, Oscar was indifferent to them. "In three months, we won't remember who they were." When El Coronel become El Presidente and photos appeared of the Presidential Couple posing with their poodles, Oscar allowed himself a moment of mild sarcasm. "The dogs look quite intelligent. An improvement over the previous cabinet."

Oscar kept his scepticism to himself. At the kitchen table, after dinner, Marta railed against El Presidente, jabbing her fat, strong fingers in the air with each phrase, "That woman! She thinks she's the Virgin Mary! His intermediary! Virgin Mary to a demagogue! A crypto-fascist! A thug! They call themselves socialists! Ha!" Oscar responded only with a half-smile, "Say what you like, but the trains run on time and that, compañera, is what counts."

When El Presidente nationalized the mines and foreign investors fled the country, Oscar gave a figurative shake of his head and imagined the day he too would flee. When La Señora went on national radio to announce a new program of public works which would be paid for by contributions from all salaried employees, Oscar wondered, "And the poodles? What will they contribute?"

When La Señora went on national radio again, this time to explain that the whole country had to be rebuilt, from the ground up, in accordance with El Presidente's national plan, and when she promised, in a voice pulsating with emotion, schools and libraries that would not, did not, materialize, Oscar felt personally insulted. "Who do they think they're fooling?" Later still, when his father was demoted for failing to make a voluntary contribution to La Señora's Fund For The Realignment Of Social Conditions, Oscar's indifference, his ironic armour, melted into a stewing pot of anger and fear.

But now she was gone and so was his ulcerous anger. In its place, he felt a slight dizziness, as if he had overstepped the bounds of moderation and drunk one too many glasses of wine. He felt pleased with himself, as if he was, somehow, at least partially, responsible for her demise. Oscar did not imagine that things would improve. El Presidente was still around and his corrupt colleagues still held posts of influence and the unions were in his pocket as was The Church. No, the country was not on the road to recovery but at least she was gone and one had to be grateful for small blessings.

The day the university re-opened, Oscar dressed in an appropriately dark suit: the official period of mourning was still in effect. When he began to knot his tie he realized he had inadvertently chosen one with a showy, florid pattern. Marta had given him this tie, which he never wore because it was too ostentatious, for his birthday two years ago. He paused and regarded himself in the mirror. Inexplicably, he continued knotting the tie. He smiled, then giggled quietly. He hopped up and down on one leg and flapped the flamboyant tie. He laughed out loud and felt possessed by an ambrosial sensation of stupidity. He made faces at himself in the mirror. "My people," he extemporized in imitation of the defunct Señora, "it is with great tenderness and a profound...awesome...indeed a profoundly awesome sense of hope for the glorious future that lies before us, a future as radiant as the light that shines out of my ass...my people, for you are my people and I am yours, I proclaim today Day Of The Audacious Necktie!"

He left the house and, despite the intense heat and high humidity, ran the twelve blocks to the bus stop, not because he was late but because he overflowed with nervous energy. The bus pulled up to the stop and, for a moment, Oscar panicked. He hesitated, inhaled slowly then released the air in a rush and at the same time took a determined step and boarded the bus. The bus driver, busy reading the newspaper, did not notice Oscar's tie. The passengers however, did. There was an audible gasp from somewhere in the crush of people and again, for a moment, Oscar felt panic. It was a stupid, pointless thing to do. Why was he calling attention to himself in this way? But it was just a tie. What harm in a tie? Oscar pressed forward and the passengers on all sides parted as if he were an untouchable. Oscar looked down at the floor of the bus, at his shoes, to hide the smile that wended its way across his lips.

The university was crumbling, ill-kept and dated from The Conquest (not the actual buildings but the content of the courses, the more disillusioned said). The classes were overcrowded; the library books mouldy; the food in the cafeteria inedible; the lighting poor and the windows, which wouldn't open, small. Most of the professors were equally dilapidated. El Presidente's active anti-intellectualism had driven many of the more capable ones into exile and those who had remained were poorly paid, tired, and, in too many cases, sadly out of touch with contemporary developments. Today, as staff and students dressed in sombre attire overwhelmed the antediluvian edifices, the university looked more melancholy than ever.

Oscar's tie flared in that pit of gloom like a neon sign for a burlesque show in a musty village church. Heads gyrated and shook; eyes popped, narrowed, blinked. Reflexively, men ran their hands over their own ties as if to haptically reassure themselves they were fittingly solemn. A young woman, a student of languages, with eyes dark and warm as chestnuts, looked directly at Oscar and smiled slowly. Oscar could not be sure if the smile signalled a sexual or political message.

The Dean of the faculty called Oscar into his cramped office. He did not ask Oscar to sit down but stood studying him for a moment. The Dean inhaled slowly through his long nostrils then said, "I don't want to know what you think. I don't want to know your opinion. I want you to go home and not come back to this school until you've changed your tie."

Oscar was about to say, "Yes sir," but the Dean stopped him with a wag of his finger.

"Nothing. Not a word please. I don't want to know."

Oscar left campus and returned home, his flagrant tie stuffed into the pocket of his jacket. But the following day, he returned to the university wearing the same tie. Once again, the Dean asked Oscar into his cramped office. This time he asked Oscar to sit down. The Dean stood looking down at Oscar. Oscar sat looking down at his tie and at his hands in his lap. Finally the Dean spoke. He said, "You are a very good student."

Oscar said nothing, he only raised his head to look at the Dean. The Dean continued, "You are, by all accounts, a serious, level-headed young man. Your professors expect you will do very well." Oscar blinked in response.

"Are you," the Dean asked, "in some kind of trouble? Please answer only with a yes or a no."

"No."

"Has someone put you up to this?" he asked, waving cautiously at the tie.

"No."

"You are, of course, entitled to your opinions, whatever they may be. You are entitled to your opinions, but you are not entitled to put this school, its staff and students, at risk because of those opinions. I make no comment on the nature of your feelings, you understand. I will ask you once again to go home and dress appropriately if you wish to attend classes. Please, Oscar. If you appear again in your present condition, you understand there is nothing I can do. Do you understand?"

"I understand."

Oscar went home and lied to his family about his day. "Fine, everything fine. The usual." That night he dreamt that he and the young woman with the eyes like chestnuts danced on the hood of an improbably long North American car. She kissed him. Her lips tasted of sea salt. Her mouth was full of wildflowers. He awoke with an emptiness in his stomach. He waited until everyone had left the house and then got out of bed. He ate nothing for breakfast. He dressed slowly. "Enough," he told himself. "There are more important things to worry about." He regarded the lurid tie hanging over the back of the chair. "A tie," he thought. "A harmless little tie. Why are we so afraid of a tie?"

He picked it up by one end and wiggled it. "See? It can't hurt you. It's a tie. My tie. Goddamn you all."

Feeling helpless, he knotted the tie and set off for school.

The communists, who had been driven underground by El Presidente and La Señora, were the first to seize on the revolutionary potential of Oscar's tie. On this third day, the same day that Oscar arrived at the university feeling sick, weak, as if he might faint, his head pounding, his tongue a dry insect in his mouth, on this day the communists showed up wearing, naturally, red ties. Arguments arose immediately. The Maoists, the Leninists, the Trotskyites and the dozen other splinter groups denounced each other as reactionary, bourgeois crypto-capitalist elements who had subverted the struggle and the symbol of the revolution. Oscar expected to be called into the Dean's office along with the fifteen communists but nothing happened. No one said anything; no one was forcibly removed from the campus.

The following day the university was in full sartorial rebellion, and within a week a critical mass had been achieved among the population of the capital. People were seen on the street, in stores, waiting in lines to buy stamps, in taxis and buses, wearing clothes that could in no way be considered appropriate for a nation in mourning. Soon it seemed the entire capital was aglow with illicit neckties and illegal hem lines. Fights broke out as some people took umbrage at the perceived assault on the memory of La Señora. Arrests were made. But overwhelmingly the populace seemed ready to defy the authorities with two-tone shoes, fire engine red dresses, hair ribbons, even bow ties. In this explosion of emotion, defiance and colour, Oscar now cut a rather ordinary figure. He put away his loud tie and took to dressing as he had in the past: soberly. "While Rome burns," he thought. "Where is this getting us? Nowhere."

The euphoria and defiance was not limited to clothing. Soon, hard be-bop jazz could be heard on radio stations and in bars. Spontaneous poetry recitals were given from balconies and public monuments. Dadaist graffiti began to appear on the city walls urging: "Coca-Cola for President," or "Give me liberty or give me liberty." There were rumours of an impending general strike. Without La Señora, it seemed, El Presidente had lost his power to control. The nation's population, once a cohesive, obeisant whole, was now a fractured, chaotic jumble.

The military coup came fast and hard. Oscar, on his way out one morning, found himself swept up by a mob thrashing its way toward the city centre. They had come from all the poor neighbourhoods of the city and from the shantytowns that ringed the capital: men, women and children, choleric and frightened. "What's wrong? What happened?" Oscar shouted as frantic hands pulled him into the wave of bodies.

"A coup!"

"We have to save the president!" screamed a voice from behind.

He looked around and saw that the men and women in the crowd carried weapons: pitchforks, shovels, picks, hammers, screwdrivers, knives, lengths of rope, brooms. "This is too sad to be true," thought Oscar, "but of course it is true. Too true. Too sad." Oscar was pressed in, mashed against elbows and legs, unable to control his movement. He could not determine where his body ended and another began. His breathing became part of the mob's and his heart, he was sure, now pumped to the meter determined by the crowd. The noise and shouting grew more and more deafening, and numerous times Oscar was lifted off his feet and carried several metres forward or back without harm as the mob shifted and reorganized.

The human wave pressing inexorably towards the city centre, towards the Presidential Palace, was subsumed in other waves pouring in from other avenues and finally, all the bodies, heaving to one furious, fearful pulse, spilled into the Plaza de la Libertad. There, at the south end of the Plaza, was the Presidential Palace where it was rumoured El Presidente was holed up. Between the mob and their president stood lines of heavily armed soldiers. Behind the soldiers, tanks. Overhead, military jets tore the morning sky to shreds.

The crowd stopped. The soldiers waited. Later, Oscar would remember how everything seemed to pause at that moment, even the breeze, how the flags all drooped and how he had to remind himself to inhale. Silence and expectation hung over the plaza. Then someone threw a rock. Oscar ran.

Rumours flew like crows. El Presidente had left the country days before. He was hidden in the American Embassy, protected by the CIA. He was hidden in the Soviet Embassy, protected by the KGB. He had died of a heart attack, of heart ache. He had gone to Switzerland to seek the aid of the United Nations. He had gone to Haiti to seek the aid of Papa Doc and powerful Rosicrucian voodoo practitioners. The only indisputable facts were the bullet holes in the walls of the Chamber of Deputies.

A General no one had heard of announced on the radio that the Armed Forces had intervened "in our historic capacity as protector of the Nation, saving the country from lawlessness, decadence and the children of La Señora and Marx." The general, who had studied hard under his U.S. instructors at the School of the Americas, explained that the military would quickly punish the malfeasants and work vigorously to restore the honour of the country.

Three days later, at eighteen minutes to four in the morning, Oscar was thrown out of bed by two men carrying guns. Someone threw a hood over his head. He heard his mother and father shouting, and something that might have been a gunshot or a car backfiring. He was pushed into a car and made to lie on the floor. Incredibly, Oscar found himself thinking about the car, how smoothly it ran, how stable it felt. Probably a Ford Falcon. He felt a boot on his neck, smelled a cigarette burning and heard two voices arguing about directions. Oscar noted the disinterested tone, the boredom in those voices, and felt a tremor run from the boot on his neck along his spinal cord to his testicles. He felt like vomiting but stopped himself because he was wearing a hood.

He was beaten with fists, boots, rubber hoses, truncheons and then questioned.

"Are you an anarchist?"

"No."

"Don't lie. Your father is an anarchist."

"No, he's not."

"He's mentioned twice in police records. Why?"

"He refused to pay bribes."

"Who was he trying to bribe?"

"He wasn't."

"Don't lie." Another blow. "Your sister is an anarchist. You are an anarchist."

"My sister? Marta...."

"We have her in custody."

"You're lying." Another blow.

"You tried to overthrow the government."

"I don't care about the government."

"An anarchist. Who else is in the 24th of July Movement?"

"Never heard of it."

"Don't lie. Your sister is part of that movement. Anarcho-syndicalists. Who do you know? Who do you answer to?"

"No one."

"Why did you participate in the attack on the Presidential Palace?"

"I didn't."

A photograph was shoved under his face. A crowd. There in the crowd, circled, his face distorted by fear. "Don't lie." Another blow.

"You are an agent provocateur."

"I'm not."

"You gave the signal."

"What signal?"

His tie was waved in his face.

"It's just a tie."

"And Marx is just a Jew son of a bitch."

"Who gave you the tie?"

Silence. A blow.

"Who gave you this tie?"

"It was a birthday present. That's all."

Another blow. Oscar looked into the eyes of the man interrogating him and felt terribly tired. Here, in the thin, pale man across from him, was a stupidity and an evil greater than La Señora and her husband. He cursed his fortune and, though not a believer, offered a brief prayer for his unhappy country.

"Who gave you the tie?"

When it became clear that Oscar wouldn't tell them who gave him the tie, he was shot in the head. One of the soldiers had suggested strangling him with it but the officer in charge of the interrogation dismissed the suggestion as "poetic and inefficient." His body, along with several others, was heaved into a pit in a garbage dump. His tie, pinned by a heap of soggy newspapers and flapping in the wind, looked like a patch of ragged wildflowers.

A Day In The Life
Of Thomas Macomber

He's trying to get it right so he can explain it later. On the screen people wander through a field of trash. They live off the garbage dump. They pick through stuff in the dump and sell it. Or use it. Or something. They live there, on the dump. Or maybe not quite on the dump. It's hard to tell exactly because they're talking Spanish or Mexican or whatever and it's hard to read the words of the translation of what they're saying. Subtitles. That's what they're called. Sometimes the subtitles disappear against the background. Or maybe his eyes are going. Doubtful with all the pot he smokes. That's good for your eyes. Glaucoma. Or something. Terminal eye patients get dope as medicine. Totally. So it can't be his eyes. It's the subtitles. They should invent some kind of system where the subtitles change colour depending on the colour that's in the background. He should invent it. Make a lot of money if you could do something like that. Like if the garbage dump is brown, then the subtitles could be the opposite colour.

"What's the opposite of brown?"

No answer.

It's somewhat of a downer this TV program. Or maybe it's the dope. Lately, whenever he tokes up, Tom gets depressed. Of course, watching documentaries about garbage dump dwellers doesn't help. It's fucking terrible. Like all those panhandlers on the street now. You can hardly turn around without bumping into somebody who's bumming for change. And every other person who isn't panhandling is rooting through the garbage or recycling, looking for beer bottles or whatever. There were like fourteen Indians in the alley the other day, looking for bottles. But they lost out cause old Mrs. Chow was already through them all at like five in the morning. With two giant bags on a pole that she carried across her back. That's why he prefers to drive. Avoid the panhandlers.

"Dad, I wanna dig a grave for Rascal."

"Jesus Bobby, you scared the crap out of me." The kid's gotten really quiet lately. Taking to sneaking around. He just shows up in the room, like a ghost. Freaky.

"Can we bury Rascal today?"

"What?"

"Can we bury Rascal today?"

"Hey, what's the opposite of brown?"

"Daaaad."

"What?"

"Can we?"

"What?"

"Bury Rascal."

"Where's your mum?"

No answer. Spooky.

Bobby is training. He is getting better and better at slipping in and out of rooms, houses, yards and conversations unnoticed. The ninja, Bobby knows, is a master of stealth and secrecy, silent as a cat, leaving no trace of his passage. Inside his kangaroo jacket pocket, he feels for his shuriken: deadly throwing stars, often coated with poison, favoured by the ninja. Nine of them. An auspicious number.

The Old Man is getting slower, Bobby thinks. Stupider too. From all the dope he smokes. It will not be long now before The Tong comes. Bobby will not defend The Old Man. He will not be sad when they take him, cut off his head and stick it on a yari for all to see. The ninja is loyal to no one but himself. Stupid Old Man.

Ninja Bobby sits on his front step watching ordinary people walk by. He could kill them with a soundless flick of his wrist. But he doesn't.

It would be something like when they colour in old movies. Colourizing. They could do the same thing with the subtitles. You do the regular subtitling. Then you go back and colourize them. But you could do it way simpler now. With computers. You just program when to change the colour depending on when the background changes and it does it automatically. It's so simple. He's amazed no one's thought of it until now.

That would be so much better than the way they work now. And also better than movies that are dubbed. That's the worst, when their mouths are moving and it's so obviously not what they're saying that you're hearing. That looks retarded. On the TV, a dog is making funny faces. He loves this commercial. He laughs.

"What's so funny?" Lori asks, dragging shopping bags into the house.

"Hey, where have you been?"

"I went to the bank."

"In what city?"

"In this city, goof. I had other stuff to do too. What's so funny?"

"It's that commercial with the mental dog that—"

She comes into the living room.

"Tom. This place is a dump."

"What?" He was supposed to clean up the living room. That's why he was in here in the first place. Now he remembers. Shit.

"The living room is a dump. I asked you when I left to clean it up. Look, you got your shit everywhere."

"It's not everywhere. It's not just my stuff."

"I asked you. Jesus. It's not much to ask."

Flick. The first shuriken goes flying. Deadly accuracy. The man crumples silently to the ground.

"What the hell have you been doing all afternoon then?"

"I've been watching this doc—It's really interesting. People living off—Look, it's the weekend. It's a day off. I'll get around to it."

Flick. Another shuriken. Another dead body. A ninja feels no pity, no remorse, no sorrow.

"When?"

"Jesus, what's the hurry? I'll do it now."

"My sister's coming over. That's all."

"Well, I didn't know that."

"You did so. I told you about eighteen times."

"You did not." She did so.

"I did so."

"No, you didn't. I think I'd remember that."

Outside, the sidewalk is littered with dead bodies. Ninja Bobby turns his back on the carnage, calmly walks past the squabbling Old People to his bed chamber. They do not notice him. To empty his mind, Ninja Bobby draws in his notebook. A city scene: roads, cars.

"Did you get rid of Rascal?"

"What?"

"Did you at least bury the dog?"

"Hey, don't yell at me."

"You didn't, did you? I told you, I'm sick of having that dog in my freezer."

"Hey, stop yelling. People can hear you, you know."

"Is Bobby home?"

"Yeah. I don't know. I guess. Bobby?"

She shushes him. "Don't call him, you idiot. I didn't know he was home. I wouldn't've talked about the dog like that if I knew he was home. D'ya think he heard me?"

"Probably. The whole city probably heard you."

Ninja Bobby adds houses and apartment buildings to his drawing. Stores, people walking, birds in the sky. Construction in one corner.

Inexplicably, Tom finds himself in the kitchen. Did he already clean up the living room? Why doesn't he do things like he says he will? He unpacks the groceries she bought. Cookies. Excellent.

"Would you leave that? Go clean up the living room."

"I'm just trying to help." Crumbs fall from his mouth.

"You can help by cleaning up the living room. And then you can bury Rascal. I told you yesterday I wanted him out of the freezer and I told Bobby we could bury him in the backyard."

"I think he was asking something about that."

"Of course, I told him we could do it."

27

"In the backyard?"

"Yeah."

"Is that...." He searches for the right word. He searches for a long time. "Safe?"

"Safe? Of course it's safe." She hates the sound of her voice, cannot stand the way she sounds. But she has no energy to change it. Not now. Maybe later. Maybe tonight. Maybe tomorrow.

"Well, what if something digs it up?"

"What, like a voodoo guy?"

"Yeah, make a zombie."

They're smiling at each other now.

"Rascal, you are a zombie. Your soul is mine to command. Go piss on Mrs. Chow's cabbage."

They're laughing now. Bobby cannot hear them. He is finishing his drawing. A Chinese Crested (a rare, hairless breed) rushes out into the busy street and is crushed under the wheels of a car that does not stop. Two blocks away, a little boy is looking for the dog. The little boy goes in the wrong direction and finds the dog much, much later. On the boulevard. He draws the person, a Good Samaritan, who stopped to check the dog and remove him from the road. The Good Samaritan is in her car seeing the accident. She can see it happening because she has long lines of sight coming straight out of her eyes. All seeing, alert.

Tracy, Lori and Tom sit in the back yard, drinking beer. The sun is low enough to be in their eyes. Tracy is talking.

"It's one of the sacred places of the planet."

"Oh yeah?" Tom shields his eyes so he can see her better.

"Uh huh. Paul has this book with all the sacred places and it's in there. I'm totally excited to be going. It has amazing energy, right? I mean spiritual energy?"

"Cool." Tracy has nice tits. He can see her bra. It's shiny, pretty. She's smiling.

"Sacred for whom?" Lori asks, putting an extra hum on the final phoneme.

"For everybody."

"What makes it sacred? I mean why is it in this book?"

"Well, it's a book of all these special places, these sacred spaces, on the planet, and it's one of them."

"Right." Tom is smiling and nodding like one of those dolls with the springy heads. At least he tidied the living room.

"Is this one of the UN places?"

"What?"

"One of the places, you know, World Heritage Places, designated by the UN?"

"The UN?"

"The United Nations?"

"Yeah, I know what the UN is Lori."

"What difference does it make if the UN says it's designated?" Tom asks.

"I'm just asking. I'm trying to understand."

"What's to understand?" Tracy finishes her beer. "It's this gorgeous place with great energy."

"Yeah, what more do you need to know?" Tom agrees.

"Maybe it's a sacred burial ground."

"Oh," Tracy jumps. "Bobby where did you come from?"

29

"My little ninja," Lori smiles and brushes the hair from his eyes. He pulls away.

"Mom. Don't."

"Hi Bobby. How are you?"

"Hey Aunty Trace. Where's Uncle Paul?"

He's not really your uncle. He hates that: Uncle Paul. What is it? It's 'cause he's not around, so he's special. It's way easier to be an uncle than a father. Fathers have to do all the crap stuff. Uncles just cruise in whenever, birthday, Christmas, take you for a ride on their motorcycle and that's it. Pals forever.

"Oh, he's working tonight."

"Is he coming by to get you later?"

"No, I've got the car."

"You want a burger, Bobby?"

"Not hungry," he growls and walks away slowly.

"Gosh he's cute. Getting so big," Tracy says.

"Yeah, he's growing up." A silence settles with the sunlight.

"Hey, you guys want to smoke a mighty doob?" Tom asks this as much to break the silence as out of desire for more.

"Mmmm. Sure." Tracy smiles. "If I can have another beer."

"You got it."

Inside the house he can hear Tracy and Lori laughing. About what? Sisters. There is a strange thing there. Something he is not privy to, something he does not know or understand. Maybe he left the spliff on the bookshelf.

"Are we gonna bury Rascal?"

"Jeeeezuz, Bobby. You can't do that. You gotta make some noise when you walk. What?"

"When can we bury Rascal?"

"I don't know. Tomorrow?"

"Tonight."

"No, not tonight. We have company."

"Aunty Trace won't mind."

"Tomorrow." He finds the joint and goes into the kitchen to get more beer. "Hey," he calls out the back door, "what's the opposite of brown?"

Tom and Lori walk down to the curb to see Tracy off. Lori leans in the car window, still talking. Tom hangs back, his hands in the pockets of his shorts. They wave goodbye when Tracy drives away and then turn around to return to the house. Bobby is standing there. Holding something in his arms. The dog.

"Bobby."

"I want to bury him."

"Honey," Lori says, "it's late now. We'll do it tomorrow."

"You said we'd do it today."

"I know honey, but."

"I wanna do it now. He needs to be buried properly."

"Okay." Lori says.

Somehow, Tom does the digging even though it was Lori that agreed. He moves two large rocks with his hands. The only light comes from the back porch and Bobby insists on lighting candles. He sings a strange little song and shuttles to and fro around the burial site.

"Shit. This is—I don't know if this is deep enough."

"Six feet under," Bobby says. "It must be six feet."

"I'm not digging six feet."

"Rascal, oh my Rascal, we bestow your body to this ground," Bobby says. Lori wonders where he gets these things. Tom watches Bobby, normally withdrawn, suddenly expressive, his face alive with something: ceremony, mystery? Kids are wild.

"Now raise the candle," Bobby commands. Tom bends over, groans, picks up the candle in its holder. It throws irregular shadows across the boy's face and the plastic wrapped dog's body he holds in his arms. He was a sweet little dog. His nails skittered across the linoleum. He could jump like nobody's business. Poor thing. Bobby climbs into the hole, places the body in the centre of the pit, then climbs back out. He crouches by the side of the hole, says, "Bye-bye Rascal."

Tom throws a clod of earth in. It falls against the plastic. Tom shivers. He throws another shovelful in. He feels sad. Why did the dog have to die? He feels stupid. Maybe it's the doob. Another mouthful of dirt. He's crying. It's been a sad day. The whole day, though he can't remember why. Hot tears run down his nose. Stupid. Lori has gone inside so she doesn't know and the ninja crouched at his feet only stares fixedly at the dirt piling up in the hole. He pushes the dirt in quickly now, awkwardly. He's doing a lousy job of it. Well, there's no light. How're you supposed to fill in a hole when it's dark?

He pushes the dirt with his foot. It sinks. He stands a moment thinking that he doesn't want to see it in the morning, a newly dug grave in the backyard. After Bobby goes to bed, he'll put the kids' swimming pool over top of it. Bobby is still crouched, his head against his knees, one hand on the mound of dirt. He's humming quietly. Then Bobby gets up abruptly, walks away, apparently no longer interested.

"Good night Bobby," mumbles Tom. He wipes his face with his t-shirt sleeve, tosses the shovel aside. He tries to pick up the swimming pool but it is round, plastic, filled with water, and, therefore, slippery, unmanageable, and immovable. Tom grunts, curses, and flicks his hands at the pool as if dismissing it. A voice calls quietly, "Dad?"

He turns. Bobby is standing on the steps of the back porch, his little boy's chest exposed to the cool air. "Bobby."

"Thanks. For doing that."

"Oh, no problem." Tom turns back to regard the grave. "We can fix it tomorrow, pack down the earth, when there's more light. I tried to put the swimming pool on it, but maybe some grass seed would be better, eh? Or flowers?" He turns back to Bobby, hoping the boy will see his smile through the darkness. Bobby is gone, vanished silently into the house.

Tom picks up the shovel. Leans it carefully against the rickety toolshed. He goes in. He adjusts the kitchen light just so that it casts a low, warm glow and sits at the kitchen table. From upstairs he can hear Lori and Bobby talking as Bobby gets ready for bed. He can't make out what they're saying but the sound of their voices creates an agreeable murmur. He listens to them and looks at his dirty hands, rubs his index finger. For a moment he has the impression that his life is very rich and that all is as it should be.

Surveillance, or
The Uncle's Disappearance

I had an uncle who worked in Intelligence for the Armed Forces, and his function, his work, was to study surveillance photos and write reports—because a photo doesn't say anything; a photo has very little meaning until you put words to it. He sat on a hard little stool and examined photographs with a loupe over a light table. And he marked the prints with a grease pencil. And described what he saw.

What did he see? Dots, blotches, squiggles, shadows, streaks of light. These he would decipher: a jeep, a weapons cache, a lovers' rendezvous, a dog pissing on a monument, soldiers digging trenches. Sometimes what at first appeared to be a balloon held by a happy four-year-old girl in a new woollen coat with a velvet collar turned out to be the explosive used by the insurgents to blow out the electrical generators. He reviewed, corrected, went over things two or three times. He organized his findings, wrote reports. These reports were taken. Elsewhere. Upstairs. What was done with them he did not know. He had no idea.

And as the weeks became months and the photographs rolled across his light table or scattered out of manila envelopes in an unending procession, he had the impression that everything was there in these photographs. Everything that existed at present was there. The entire city, the country, every weapon and every soldier and every footpath and every runway and every last element of the war. Every everything.

He was given lists and dossiers and he worked from these. He worked from rumours that made their way to him, crumbled and precious like black market chocolate. There were rumours that the war was over. Rumours that the war had changed. Rumours that the generals and the leaders had left, slipped over the mountains. Rumours of millions siphoned off and hidden in numbered foreign accounts. Rumours of a purge. Rumours that an invasion of the capital was due. Rumours of misinformation, of black propaganda. Rumours of new and terrible weapons. Rumours of terrible crimes. Rumours.

He looked at the blurry photos and saw places and people he knew. He named the dots. He wrote it all down, blinking and sweating over his light table.

One day he found himself studying photographs of the building in which he worked. An unremarkable building, like so many in the new part of the capital, but unmistakably, the building in which he worked, studying photographs and writing reports. And as he shuffled through this stack, he saw photographs of the hallways he walked every day, photographs of the doors he opened every morning and, finally, photographs of the room in which he worked.

He circled the blotch which he identified as himself in a photograph of himself sitting hunched over the light table, pencil in hand, studying a photograph of himself studying a photograph over a light table and so on. He reported what he saw. Wrote it down. Diligent as ever. And perhaps suspecting it was a kind of test. It wasn't.

The Several Lives Of Citizen Suárez

Fernando Suárez, thirteen years old and barefoot, stood on his bed (bedspread of boats), his thin arms crossed on the window sill, head thrust out the window, studying the sky. Two pinpricks of light glinted faintly in the moonless night. He wondered what they were. He should at least be able to see the Big and Little Dipper he thought. Perhaps they were part of the Dippers, those stars. One of them might be Polaris. He couldn't tell. The firmament in his part of the world was virtually empty and consequently, unreadable.

Earlier in the day, in the library, he had looked at a map. A Map of the Heavens. An enormous blue disk, (so blue you could swim in it, sink in it, so blue it was almost black) decorated with silver stars arranged in their various and beautiful constellations. He had walked all around the map, murmuring: Cassiopeia, Andromeda, Sirius, Orion, Betelgeuse, Castor, Pollux, Canis Major and Minor. Beautiful names. Each name, each star, a story. The sky was full of stories. Castor and Pollux were twins who travelled to find the golden fleece. Cassiopeia and Andromeda were mother and daughter. He didn't know the stories in their entirety, just pieces of them, enough to render the sky mysterious and wonderful.

There were other things too. Asteroids, planets of course, meteors, and black holes. Black holes were collapsed stars. Dead stars that had imploded, fallen in on themselves. As the star collapsed, it became increasingly dense and its gravitational field became stronger and stronger until it became an invisible pit of total gravity that sucked up everything that passed by. In a black hole, a beam of light would fall back to the ground like a ball tossed into the air. Black holes were discovered by scientists working out solutions to problems developed by Einstein. No one had ever seen one; they couldn't be seen by telescopes—how do you see a black hole in the blackness of space?—but physicists had theoretical proof that they actually existed. Fernando and his friend Simon Cooper intended to be the first physicists to furnish material proof of their existence.

Fernando scanned the sky again. Maybe it was cloudy. That's why he couldn't see any stars. Or else there was a black hole moving across this part of the sky, sucking up everything around it. Could that happen? he wondered. Did black holes move? Maybe if he waited and watched carefully enough he'd see a comet or a meteor. The sky was full of meteors the books said and on clear nights you were supposed to be able to see them with the naked eye, but Fernando had never seen one. Probably you had to go out into the country, he thought.

"Pancho?" His mother called up the stairs, "*Dónde estás, mijo?*"

"In here. In my room."

"What are you doing?"

"Just looking at the stars."

"*¿Qué ves? Se ve algo?*" She sat on the corner of the bed, smoothed a wrinkle in the bedspread.

"No, I think it's too cloudy." This might be a good time to talk about the telescope, he thought. He'd been looking and there was one in the catalogue that wasn't—

"I want to talk to you about something. To ask you something." She's smiling so, Fernando thought, it can't be anything bad. Maybe after she says her thing I can ask her about the telescope. "*Sabes que Papi y yo,*" she continued, "we've been studying to become Canadian citizens." He nodded. "And this Friday, at the end of the week, is the day we go to the judge and we get our citizenship." He withdrew completely from the window, closed it and sat with a bounce on the bed.

The citizenship process was of interest to him. He had looked at the books with his parents and helped them study for the test. He knew a lot about it because they talked about some of these things in school and because, as well as his passion for physics, he was interested in things political: governments, revolutions, nation-states.

He liked the words associated with citizenship, especially the phrase "landed immigrant." It related an epic story and conveyed a special, to Fernando at least, status. It was the "landed" part of the phrase he liked best. Landed: arrived safely on terra firma after a perilous ocean journey, like his grandfather who had left Europe and gone to South America, crossing the dark and cold waters of the Atlantic in a rustbucket boat named after a princess no one remembered. Landed: like Colon, like Balboa, like Cabot, like Armstrong, like Cartier, like the Pilgrims, like the Africans, except they weren't immigrants. They were slaves.

"And we are very excited about it. We are very happy to finally be really Canadian and very proud. *Y lo que te quería decir, bueno, lo que te quería preguntar, es que nosotros podemos* on Friday *hacerte ciudadano tambien si quieres. Me entiendes?* We can also get your citizenship for you at the same time. Because you are a minor we can ask the judge to give you your citizenship with our citizenship."

Fernando imagined the proceedings. A judge sat at a large desk, behind him a Canadian flag, a framed photograph of the Queen, and that shield with the unicorn or lion on it. His parents stood below the judge, looking up. The judge banged his gavel (Fernando did not know this word; he called it 'that wooden hammer that judges use') and then smiled, congratulated his parents and handed them a piece of paper. His parents were very happy. He could not see himself anywhere in this picture.

"I'll be a citizen too?"

"Yes."

"Then I won't be a landed immigrant anymore?"

"No, you'll be a Canadian citizen *con pasaporte Canadiense.*"

It had never occurred to Fernando that he too might become Canadian. "And what about my other passport?"

"You wouldn't use that anymore."

"But what about my other citizenship?"

"Well, you still keep that. You never lose that. We'll have dual citizenship."

Dual citizenship sounded interesting. Sounded unique. "But I'd be a Canadian."

"*Si mijo.*"

"I don't think I want to have my citizenship, *mamí.*"

"*Porqué no?*"

"I don't want to be a Canadian."

"*Pero, porqué no?*"

"*No sé.* I don't want to."

His mother's gaze was gentle. She noticed the sudden tightness in his mouth and his arms crossed on his lap ended in small fists. She saw his brown eyes flicker with worry.

"*Bueno*," she said. "Okay. I want you to think about this. I want you to tell me *porqué* you don't want your citizenship and if you can give me a good reason then you don't have to. Okay?"

"Now, I have to tell you?"

"No, not now. Before Friday. You have *hasta* Thursday night. Okay?"

"Okay."

She gave him a kiss and left the room.

Lina Suárez, vivacious, well dressed, slim—not that she watched her weight particularly, she simply had, as she said, "*un metabolismo muy* fast"—walked down the carpeted stairs unaware that she puckered her lips. She always puckered her lips when she thought. Perhaps she should have explained to Fernando all the advantages that Canadian citizenship conferred. But he knew those things; they had discussed them many times. She might have mentioned the troubles, the disturbances, back home and how a Canadian passport would give Fernando some security against those problems. But Fernando knew something of that too and it was best not to linger on those things; it would only worry him unnecessarily. She recognized that Fernando's reaction was not uncharacteristic; he was sensitive, Fernando, emotional. Where she and her husband considered almost all things rationally, mathematically perhaps—her husband was a statistician after all—Fernando usually responded intuitively, emotionally. And certainly he had very strong feelings about who he was and where he came from.

For Lina, citizenship, and the passport that was its token, was the conclusion of a long and difficult journey. Whereas her husband—she thought of him as 'my husband,' not Octavio—had settled into his new life in Canada with great facility, almost as simply as changing a pair of trousers, for Lina the transition had been violent, upsetting. Of course he'd had his position to anchor him as well as the familiar, minor comforts of university life to ease his passage. Lina had only her determination to succeed and the attentions of a worried little boy who relied on her.

That first winter had been terrible. Months and months of silence. The cold was nothing compared to the silence the snow imposed. Snow that appeared so delightful in pictures was in reality—at least the reality of those distended months—oppressive and discomforting. Unrelieved, stifling whiteness that dampened everything till no footstep, no voice, no sound of human endeavour could be heard. The features of the terrain, minimal as they were in the suburb they had settled in, were reduced to insignificance by the snow. Tree, tricycle, hedge, car, doghouse, all became equally indecipherable undulations in the interminable whiteness.

She cried often and furtively that first year. After, she would reprimand herself for her sentimental attachment to the flowering lemon trees and the noisy birds which gathered in that particular garden on the other side of the world. She told herself that it was only a matter of time, that one could adapt to all sorts of things, that she was being weak, that her husband would not approve. She told herself that she had to set an example for the boy.

Fernando had his tears and anxieties too. Once a gregarious toddler, he had suddenly become illogically fearful of strangers. When approached by anyone speaking English, Fernando would put his hands over his ears and shake his head, "*No no no. Asi no. No quiero. No.*" If they persisted he would run away and sometimes collapse around his mother's ankles, sobbing and wailing. Lina tried to be patient. She tried to make him see that the strangers were kind and friendly but Fernando would only say that he didn't want them, and when pressed to tell her who or what he did want, he would answer, "Nona."

Lina wanted Nona, her mother, too but she didn't tell Fernando that. It was unrealistic. Impossible at the moment. Nona was far away she'd tell Fernando. "We live in Canada now and we have to try to get along with these people. We have to speak English. Like Papí. Papí speaks English all day." Fernando didn't want to speak English. He didn't want new friends. He didn't like the nice strangers. *No, no, no quiero. No quiero.*

There were days when Lina could not endure Fernando's tears and whining. She would lose her temper eventually and slap him, telling him sharply to stop stop stop. Then she would shut him in his room until he resolved to be sensible. Fernando, a sensitive boy, could sense the agitation his outbursts created. He saw his mother struggle with a grief of her own and, alone in his room, longed for her to be happy and gentle again. When he emerged, quiet and pale, eyes downcast, she was always very gentle and tried to cheer him. She'd take him on her lap and cuddle him, smooth and kiss his hair, make hot chocolate *caliente*. He was a good boy really, such a good boy, and it was hard, she knew how hard it was, but they just had to get used to it.

Her husband, Octavio, was also not unaware of her struggle to adjust. He was solicitous and patient. He took his family out for drives in the country and encouraged Lina to get out and take some English classes, not so much to improve her English but to meet people. He tried to get to know the neighbours but none of them seemed interested in reciprocating the effort and he didn't really have that much time. He had a great deal of work to do at the university and, because he was new and foreign, a great deal to prove.

Once, on an excursion into (the disappointingly small, big-city of) Toronto, they found a store called, simply enough, *El Almacén* that carried, as promised on the awning, *Productos Latinos*. Fernando found it. He heard music, a voice singing in Spanish, and had dashed into the store to be closer to the source. The store sold week-old newspapers, magazines, records and cassettes, some specialty food items, coffee, tea, soft drinks, key tags, and plastic flags in various sizes. Though the proprietor was a Peruvian, Lina and Octavio were very pleased to have stumbled upon the store. They spoke animatedly and at length with the man, surprised by their enthusiasm for and enjoyment of a conversation about shopkeeping. Fernando sat below them, in front of a glass display case, listening, transported with delight. They bought a newspaper, a cassette, (the music that was playing when Fernando rushed in) and some chocolate. Fernando was distraught when they tried to leave and clung pathetically to the display case. His father was forced to pry his slender fingers off the glass to get him out of the store.

Lina heard her husband clanging about in the garage. She wouldn't bother him with this particular development. Her husband relied on her to attend to the domestic sphere and she knew he appreciated her ability to keep him apprised of household matters without overwhelming him with the minutiae of domestic life. She felt satisfaction, proud of the distance, literal and metaphoric, she and her family had travelled. Her husband was an associate professor, certain to be made a full professor in a few years; she worked part-time at a bank, not because she needed to but because she liked to; and Fernando was an excellent student who now spoke English much better than he did Spanish. They had a lovely home in a very good neighbourhood, a new car, and they sent money home regularly. If they weren't entirely happy, well, nothing ever worked out exactly as planned and who, after all, was entirely happy?

***

After school Fernando told Simon that he had some things to think about and that he wanted to be alone.

"Math?" Simon asked.

"No." Fernando shook his head and looked off into the horizon.

"Physics?"

"No, family stuff," Fernando told him.

"Oh." They stood facing but not looking at each other for a moment. Fernando kicked a small stone which landed at Simon's feet.

"Sorry," he mumbled.

"What is it?"

"I don't really want to talk about it." And then because Simon looked injured by Fernando's rejection he added, "It's sort of private? Family stuff. You know?"

"Sure, "Simon nodded. "See you tomorrow or call me tonight. Hey did you see Heidi today? Ohmigod her boobs are getting huge. She's gotta be stuffing. Call me tonight okay?" He walked off quickly, hands jammed into the pockets of his jacket in imitation of his older brother.

Fernando lingered at the perimeter of the playground until all the younger children had abandoned the equipment and then climbed into the red plastic tube that connected the twisty slide to the climbing apparatus. He sat with his knees around his ears and his back arched to conform to the shape of the tube. He slapped the sides and hummed softly to feel the resonance. He poked at the toes of his running shoes. He wished he were younger. Little kids had no problems. No real problems. No substantial decisions to make.

Fernando knew he did not want Canadian citizenship. He knew that immediately and with great certainty only moments after his mother had made the suggestion. Fernando was not, he was convinced, constituted as a Canadian. His guts were foreign. His lungs were a deviant shape; his nose sensitized to other aromas and flavours. His ear was pitched to other frequencies; his cranial-sacral rhythm was governed by a divergent drummer. And Spanish, though he spoke it less and less, altered the tides of his blood, modified his circadian rhythms. It told him things only he could comprehend. (Years later, after watching him speak Spanish with a stranger in a store, a girlfriend would remark: I understood something about you just now.)

The idea of accepting Canadian citizenship seemed a profound betrayal of various people: his Nona; his grandfather Rafael; his other grandfather, Mario; and the beggar boy at the café that afternoon in the capital.

Fernando remembered. A boy his age had appeared at the table where they sat eating lunch (overhead, the dark wooden blades of a fan rotated slowly, ominously) and asked if he could have one of the sandwiches they were eating or one of the sodas they were drinking and when Fernando's father gently shook his head no, the boy asked if he could have some of the sugar packages on the table. Fernando said nothing then and only mentioned it once, much later, to Simon: a boy, our age, on the street, he came up and asked for a sandwich to eat. He thought about it obsessively. He believed he was related to the boy in some way. They were, he was sure, connected, associated.

Because black holes were enormous tangles in space-time, scientists and mathematicians believed they could be paths into other universes. Some scientists thought it was possible that in these other universes there might be people, our doubles, leading lives almost exactly like ours. Fernando thought that perhaps something like that had happened with the beggar boy. The boy was Fernando in some way, the boy Fernando might have become if they hadn't emigrated perhaps. The boy was a version of Fernando from another universe and the two of them had intersected somehow. He did not have the math to prove it of course, nor the language with which to arrange his ideas, but it was what he felt.

His position as a foreigner and his knowledge of the double or perhaps multiple lives he lived was for him a recondite and marvellous wound. It was both light and pain, darkness and delight. His selfhood was a delirious lesion which, when palpated mentally, throbbed with a transcendental anguish that included a measure of triumph.

Fernando thought of the penitents who marched on bleeding knees, scourging their backs with thick ropes—an image he had unearthed reading about Seville after his mother had mentioned her father was born there—mortifying their flesh, joyously offering up their suffering to God. He had asked his mother about it and she had explained what she could, carefully adding that really it was a superstitious practice. If there was a god, she said, he probably didn't demand such extreme behaviour from his followers. Fernando noted the tone of disapproval in her voice and was careful from then on to always refer to *Semana Santa* and the more extreme elements of Catholicism with a note of distaste but in truth he was fascinated and, as far as he was concerned, a universe that contained things as bizarre as black holes surely had room for a penitent or two.

He felt afraid: afraid that something would be taken from him, lost to him, if he were to renounce his gift in exchange for the normalcy citizenship conferred. What he would lose he couldn't say; he knew only that he would lose.

***

Octavio Suárez's intermittent affair with Veena Dubai— seven years his junior, assistant professor, the only woman (apart from the receptionist) in the department and the only other person, as they jokingly put it, "not-from-here"—had entered a waxing phase. Octavio Suárez believed that what he most admired was order, but this business with Veena— he thought in such euphemisms—upset his convictions about himself and made him question whether he had led his life according to all the wrong principles.

When they met Octavio had been entranced by her enormous, dark eyes (his wife's were small, sharp and closely set), her lustrous hair and extravagant figure. She, in turn, liked his refined manner, his slim hips and neat white teeth. She liked his softly accented, and slightly old-fashioned, English. They had fallen (literally) into bed very quickly one rainy evening after he had driven her home from a meeting. Lying on her bed, his clothing scattered across the broadloom, Veena a warm and dark wave above him, Octavio felt as if he had fallen into a fog, an irresistibly compelling stupor in which he had no power over his actions. Afterwards, he felt numb, shocked by what had occurred, and told himself it was a terrible mistake never to be repeated, but nonetheless, found himself, inexplicably, comparing Veena's breasts to the domes of a mosque. The comparison was inexplicable because he was sure he had never seen a mosque other than in National Geographic and in any case, he believed Veena was Hindu and not Muslim and therefore, the more apt comparison would have been with a temple. But temples didn't have domes. Or at least he didn't think they did. He couldn't recall ever having seen a Hindu temple either, though, he thought, he must have at some point.

When he got home, he called a hasty hello from the garage entrance and ducked into the washroom on the main floor. He washed his face and hands then undid his shirt to wash his upper body, paying special attention to his underarms. He brushed his teeth as well, using only a speck of toothpaste because too fresh a mouth would have been unusual. He nervously kissed his wife on the shoulder and announced he was extremely tired and going to bed immediately. She did not, as far as he knew, suspect anything. He lay in bed consumed by equal parts of remorse and amazement.

After that first tumble, Veena and Octavio contrived to find themselves together often. They didn't talk much; they had sex. Veena appreciated that Octavio took his time and

Octavio was exhilarated by her open enjoyment of the act—another of his euphemisms. His wife was obliging and pleasant in bed but her smiles and soft osculations could not compare with Veena's muscular and demanding lovemaking. They enjoyed one another for some months until Veena announced she did not want to be the other woman anymore. Octavio replied, with some relief, that he understood perfectly.

Lina, of course, noticed the change. Her husband suddenly had more time. He no longer worked so late. He wasn't always irritable and tired. He was very kind to her again. She said nothing and told herself that love was sometimes tested in these ways and that the important thing was that he had stayed with her. She responded to her husband's kindness and took extra interest in his accounts of inter-departmental squabbling and politics. Octavio told himself that his wife was a good woman, a fine wife, a good mother. Truly, the business with Veena was isolated, exceptional, never to be repeated.

But there was no reason why he and Veena couldn't be civil, polite, even friendly with one another. They were, after all, colleagues. They took coffees together, chatted in hallways, shared small jokes during departmental meetings and discussed problems they had with students and other faculty members. At a meeting early in the following academic year, Octavio found himself gazing with nostalgic fondness at the thick black hair that curled down and caressed the back of Veena's neck. Perhaps she experienced his gaze as a subtle and warm pressure because she turned to him after the meeting and asked, in a voice tottering on the edge of laughter, if he would drive her home. He stammered, "Yes, certainly," nodded his head vigorously, and, abruptly, they became entangled again.

They were reckless this time: taking long walks around the campus, sitting together under the shade trees and describing to each other the landscapes, sounds, smells, and tastes of their lives "back home." They shared meals and drank in squalid bars on the fringes of town. They kissed openly in his car, caressing each other like teenagers. They made love in his cramped office once, against, and finally, on the desk. It was awkward and uncomfortable but spectacularly exciting.

Veena, however, grew alarmed by Octavio's increasingly frequent references to divorce and broke off with him again, initiating a relationship with a young doctor she had met at a Progressive Conservative party fundraising dinner.

Veena's departure brought Octavio back to his senses—that was the phrase he used to describe the situation to himself—and he set out to repair any damage this latest sleep of reason had created in his marriage. He announced to his wife and son that they were going home. For a visit. It had been eight years since they had left and in that time, though they often talked of and wrote home—Lina did anyway, signing cards and letters for both of them—they had never discussed the possibility of returning for a visit.

It was an exhausting vacation, menaced by emotional expectations and demands on all sides. Octavio and Lina suffered under the strain of maintaining a solid, cheerful front for their families. Fernando helplessly and unknowingly metabolized all the unvoiced tension and uneasiness which fermented in the ether surrounding his parents, aggravating his already excitable condition. He spent much of the vacation on the verge of tears. Everything he saw, heard, smelled, and touched was fraught with tenderness and need. He felt that his relatives—and there were so many he did not remember—needed him to respond to them affectionately. They expected kisses, hugs, caresses. They wanted him to tell them stories, sing, recount his life in Canada, teach them words in English and share in every detail of their lives. And Fernando wanted to. He desperately wanted to love them. But he couldn't. Not all at once. Not right away.

He became by turns petulant, demanding, withdrawn, bullying. He resented the demands made of him and at the same time despised himself for being so miserly with his affection. He saw himself behaving horribly and did not know what to do. This self-knowledge and impotence only increased his unhappiness.

Desperation occluded even his response to his Nona. She showered him with candies and affection and treated him too much like the young child she had known. Only with Nona's husband—they weren't, in fact, married: another cause for tension—a man Fernando had not known previously, Mario, did he feel comfortable enough to let his guard down. Mario played chess with the boy on the bougainvillaea-scented balcony every afternoon, made him ice cream, slipped cognac into his hot chocolate, took him for walks, and made few demands except that Fernando pay more attention to the deployment of his knights and rooks.

To Lina and Octavio's families he appeared a sober, quiet boy, perhaps even cold. They were disappointed, hurt. He had changed. Well, they said, of course, it's been eight years. He's almost Canadian now, gone away so long. They said this within his hearing as though he were deaf or could not understand what they meant. Finally, Fernando became ill with bronchitis and was subjected to a series of humiliating injections in his buttocks. After the illness, they spent their last few days in the capital visiting friends and shopping for jewellery. Fernando wanted to buy something too but could not come to a decision till the last moment when they rushed out to find a good compass with phosphorescent markings.

Almost immediately upon their return, Octavio had sought out Veena. She listened to his sorry tale but refused his entreaty for physical consolation. She had continued to refuse his advances until only last month (after finally breaking up with Kevin Owen, the heartbroken Progressive

Conservative urologist) when they had celebratory and frantic sex in the alley behind her apartment building.

Octavio had by now almost resigned himself to this sexual thraldom. He was an educated man, modern. He recognized that sex was a powerful, primal, force. Mentally, he divided the aspects of his life. Work and family, well-lighted and centre stage in the Cartesian theatre; Veena and sex there, off in the wings: covert, occult, undeniable.

He chafed under the oppressive burden of maintaining two lives and felt, at times, like a figure in someone else's dream. His actions did not appear autonomous; he was without agency and forced to endure the capricious demands of an unseen overlord. Sometimes he imagined that he was being dragged down a lightless tunnel. At the end of the tunnel he would be asked to make a grave decision.

***

Lina Suárez's affair with Mike Green was more the product of design than chance or any other unconscious force. Lina had stopped in at the Mac's Milk convenience store in the strip mall to pick up a quart of milk and some aspirin, and was standing at the magazine rack contemplating the various publications when the lurid cover of *Terrible and True Confessions* caught her attention. A slatternly hoyden in dishabille proclaimed: I Cheated On My Hubby Again and Again and Again!—And Loved It!! Lina thought at once of the woman with whom her husband had been involved and felt shame which turned quickly to anger and then dissipated entirely as she re-read the headline.

It had, naturally, occurred to her. Revenge: an eye for an eye, a romp for a romp. But she had dismissed the whole idea as entirely embarrassing and impossible. The logistics of an affair were simply too complicated. Who? Where? When? No, it was too difficult and would prove nothing, change nothing.

The cheerful young man at the till, tall and blue eyed, nodded as she approached. He rang up her purchases.

"B.B. King," she said.

"What? Oh yeah, that's right," he said, his face brightening with surprise and turning, aetiological, to regard the tape deck behind him where the cassette played. "That's right, uh, B.B. King."

"*Live In London*," she added.

"Hey, that's right. Yeah, London." He stood there nodding and smiling at her. She smiled back. He put the milk and aspirin in a plastic bag. "You, uh, like the blues?"

"Oh, I don't know so much the blues. I like B.B. King."

"Yeah, well, he's one of the great ones that's for sure."

"Yes." There was a moment's silence. His name tag said Mike. "I am sure you like the blues, Mike."

"Oh yeah. I love the blues. I adore the blues. It's my music."

"Do you play?"

"Only the records." He laughed. She laughed. "I've got over seven hundred of 'em."

"Seven hundred records?" Yes, she decided, she was definitely flirting with him.

"Yep. Over."

"All blues?" Lina expressed mild disbelief.

"No, no, mostly blues but of course I've got R&B and Motown and some old country, real country music, oh all sorts of things but mostly, mostly I have the blues." His face expressed an idea of some gravity.

"Every day I have the blues," Lina said.

"Oh, that's too, I'm uh sorry—" he began and then realized that, incredibly, she had made a blues reference. A B.B. King reference. He laughed. "Right, everyday I have the blues. Right." He smiled with his mouth wide open such that she could see his crowned molars and a thin strand of saliva that glistened in the far reaches of the pink interior. He shook his head rapidly. "Not a lot of people.... Most people these days you know, especially around here, they're into, you know, they're not into the blues."

Hands hidden behind the counter and head inclined, casually, downward as if she were searching for something on the surface of the counter, Lina said, "I am sure you have some very good records in that collection. It must be something to see."

"Oh, I've got, I've got some, well ah...." Suddenly he could not remember a single album he owned except for the new Peter Frampton he had just bought and that certainly didn't qualify as an esoteric blues record. "Uh Pinetop Perkins, uh Honeyboy Edwards, James Cotton, Mose Allison, Mose Vinson, uh Sonny Terry—I mean—If you knew, if you saw—Would you like...?" Then he panicked slightly, "I don't mean, I mean if you're interested. I mean, you seem interested and it's not often you meet someone who uh..." and all the while he rattled the handles of the plastic bag into which he had put Lina's aspirin and milk. Two grinning teenagers (who had, only moments ago, smoked a joint behind the store) entered noisily, and he shoved the bag at Lina saying, "Thank you very much. Have a nice day."

"Hey man," one of the kids said as they stumbled down the centre aisle, "Do you have those jumbo bags of Ketchup chips?"

Lina left the store uncertain whether to laugh or rush back and apologize to the poor young man. She spent the next two days in a state of nervous tension, reviewing each nuance of the conversation and trying to determine what it might have meant. It wasn't that she was attracted to the boy in any way. It was...what? It was just an unusual exchange. Purely innocent. Maybe she wanted to hear some good blues. Maybe she didn't care about the blues at all. Maybe what she liked was the feeling of doing something wrong, even if she hadn't done anything wrong. Yet. Maybe what she liked, she sometimes thought, was how nervous she seemed to make him. She made two other trips to the store that week but Mike wasn't working.

Then, Octavio who never wore anything but a suit and tie to work, came home after "a staff meeting" one night wearing a t-shirt, a faded *Coke Is It* t-shirt. Lina, simultaneously wounded and amazed by his audacity, asked him what happened to his clothes. Stumbling only once, Octavio explained that he had spilled ink, exploded a pen, all over his shirt and had been obliged to borrow the t-shirt from—and here he paused briefly, a microsecond of a pause, barely a breath of a pause, but pause enough for Lina to know—a colleague, and he gave the name of a man who weighed at least ten kilos more than he did. "Ah," Lina responded, nodding. "Ah." Then she lit a cigarette and neglected to open a window. Octavio said nothing.

The next day she marched into the Mac's Milk, determined to wait for Mike all day if necessary. But waiting, it turned out, would not be necessary. Mike was there in his uniform and name tag, looking as milk-fed and blue-eyed as she remembered him. He blinked rapidly and brought his hands to his face in a gesture of confusion when he saw it was her; he thought of her as "that French lady." Before he could speak Lina said, "I would like to see your records, Mike. When can we arrange this?"

"Oh ah, Jeez, I don't know. Uh, whenever you like, I mean...."

"When do you finish work?"

"Today?"

"Yes, today."

"Oh, uh, well, I'll be out of here around two-thirty, three o'clock."

His apartment was an uninspired but surprisingly dust free and tidy affair that contained a brown couch, a small wooden table with four chairs, a mustard coloured fridge and an avocado green stove. There was a bowl of fruit (three Macintosh apples, one elderly Israeli orange) on the sideboard and a case of beer on the floor, along with three alienated cushions. Concert posters covered the walls. Pride of place was given to the expensive stereo and the seven hundred and forty-one (he had counted them since they last spoke) records.

Lina sat on the couch wearing headphones (the neighbours didn't appreciate good music) while he played snatches of records and offered commentaries on the artist; whom they had recorded with; how they had been ripped off by managers, record companies or other more famous musicians; where he had found the record; how much he paid for it; what it might be worth to other collectors; how he would never sell it, and so on. Lina grew cold with boredom. She asked if he had anything to drink. Other than beer, apple juice or milk, Mike only had bourbon. She sipped gingerly from the tumbler and wondered what the hell she was doing. Finally she asked Mike to show her the rest of the apartment.

"Well, there's not much more. It's not the Taj Mahal or anything." He gave a deprecatory laugh. "There's just my uh my room and the uh washroom, down that hall."

Lina realized that nothing would happen unless she took the initiative. She drank the filthy bourbon—the glass, to his credit, was spotless—in two gulps and asked him to play something they could dance to.

"You wanna dance?" If what he thought was happening was, in fact, happening then he didn't know what he was gonna do. "Fast or slow?"

"What? Sorry?" She removed a strand of hair from her mouth.

"Do you wanna dance fast or uh slow?"

"Slow."

They danced to Bobby Bland's *Stormy Monday*. She tucked in close to him and could feel his erection through his trousers. She resigned herself to the inevitable. She didn't feel too bad; the bourbon put a soft haze on everything: the room, the rhythm of the music, Mike, her feelings. I cheated on my hubby and didn't mind it. She thought it was touching that he had an erection already.

"How old are you Mike?" she asked softly, pulling her head away from his shoulder.

"Me? I'm twenty-four."

"Twenty-four," she almost smiled.

"How old are you?"

"Ah-ah-ah. No, you don't ask that," she said. When the song ended Mike moved quickly away from her and went back to the record collection as if to choose another record.

"Leave that," she said. She walked down the hall and opened the door to his bedroom. He followed her at a distance. "Well...?"

"Um, what's your name?"

"Lina."

She stood beside his bed, a single. He stood in the doorway, unsure where to look, his soft and slightly puffy hands stuffed in the back pockets of his jeans.

"That's a pretty name. You're married, aren't you?"

She walked up to him, emboldened by his timorousness and pushed his fair, thin hair out of his eyes. "What's wrong? Don't you want to?"

"Uh yeah, I do, I mean, yeah, I really do."

"So...?" She sat down now on the edge of the bed and noted that a part of her had floated free of her body to observe the proceedings from the corner of the room above the door. This part of her noted the neat, empty room: the socks and T-shirts in the laundry hamper in the corner; the large, blue glass bowl filled with pennies; the missing knob on the closet door; the particle board dresser. This part of her awareness also observed herself, smiling an indulgent, gentle smile at Mike, and did not believe what she saw. Who is that, she wondered. This isn't happening. But the watcher in the corner assured her that it really was happening.

He's a virgin, she thought when Mike suddenly loomed above her, his belt undone, unzipping his pants. Lina involuntarily turned her head away and shouted, "Wait, no. Let's turn off the lights. Pull the blind." And then more calmly, "You have prophylactics?"

"What?" He stumbled about, clutching his pants with one hand while he tangled with the venetians on the window.

"Prophylactics. Condoms. For the...."

"Oh. Uh, no." And thus was Lina's first attempt at infidelity abandoned.

But Lina was nothing if not persistent. She returned a week later with a package of condoms in her purse and three glasses of wine in her system. She declined Mike's bourbon, threw the condoms onto the table and said, "Let's do it." Mike disappeared into the bathroom and Lina went to the bedroom. A single bed. What kind of man, she thought as she undressed—she debated leaving her bra and panties on; they were very pretty but would probably be wasted on the poor boy—sleeps in a single bed? She felt absolutely no desire and tried not to think of what they were about to do. It would simply happen. It would happen and then it would be over and then...something would have changed.

And it did happen. Eventually. And something did change.

Over time, Lina began to think of Mike as an opportunity to experiment. He didn't mind being told what to do, in fact he seemed to need to be told. Soon she no longer allowed him to get on top of her and now, months later, she rarely allowed Mike to penetrate her at all, insisting instead that he masturbate himself while she watched and only sometimes allowing him to rub his penis between her breasts, an act that seemed to afford him a ridiculous degree of pleasure. For his part, Mike was beside himself. He thought he had died and gone to an issue of *Penthouse*. Lina remained ever rational; her approach was methodical, clinical and heuristic.

There was some affection between them. She helped Mike decorate his apartment, choosing new furniture and fixtures; she advised him about his clothing and hair; she talked openly about her husband, though she tried to avoid mention of Fernando. She had come to like his softness; his happy smile moved something in her. Mike took Lina to matinees of Hollywood movies Octavio would never see; he recommended good books, made her tapes and, occasionally, extemporized intriguing vegetarian meals.

Lina had no difficulty sustaining this shadowy (and smoky—Mike, unlike her husband, smoked) life and her official life. When she was with Mike, smoking, eating oranges and drinking tea, she felt that this was her life and the house where she lived with her husband and son was something else, an ill-remembered dream. On the days she did not see Mike—at home preparing dinner or discussing a school day with Fernando, the afternoons she worked at the bank—Mike and his single bed seemed like a vacation she had taken in a previous life. She slipped amphibious between the two realms and it cost her nothing to do so. Only once did she cry, and then very briefly, in his narrow bed, sorrowful and lonely, after Mike had left for work, thinking of the fruit trees, the faces and colours, the broad shaded avenues of her home, wondering, cursing that she ever ended up in this situation.

Though the idea that his parents were unfaithful to one another (or, more specifically, that his father enjoyed a young professor from behind while his mother smoked a cigarette and made the paunchy Mac's Milk store manager kneel naked in front of her before she allowed him to touch one of her breasts) never occurred to him, his parents' unhappiness preyed on Fernando silently and subtly. If a counsellor or therapist were to have asked him if his parents loved each other, Fernando would have answered, "Yes," but as the breath rose from his lungs and cautiously sounded his vocal chords and before the monosyllable rearranged itself on his tongue and lips, it would have tripped nervously on his glottis, thereby grating and irritating sensitive tissue at the back of his throat, resulting, over time, in a mild somatic disturbance, barely noted, unrecognized, unnamed, idiopathic.

Their unhappiness was sterile: dry and soundless. It was a suburban, upper-middle class unhappiness, and it went unremarked on and unnoticed by everyone, including Octavio and Lina. It revealed itself only in minor details: lack of appetite, ear and head aches, some hair loss, a garage full of abandoned projects, a television in the bedroom, mumbling, difficulty sleeping, etc.

***

As the week wore on, Fernando became increasingly preoccupied in school. "Daydreaming," his teachers said. "Fern," they cooed. Or "Earth calling Fernando." The other students laughed and Fernando reacted with a start and looked away, digging with his thumbnail at the worn grooves on the desktop, furrows in the otherwise flat topography of wood grain and ink.

After school he returned to his red tube, dejected and alone. He had made absolutely no headway; he couldn't think straight about this problem. He was overwhelmed, inundated by the inchoate notions he had of himself and his place in the order of things.

Fernando's cosmos was carefully balanced on two points, and constant attention was required to maintain that delicate, precarious equilibrium. Any false move, any favouring of one aspect over the other, would result, or so he imagined, in catastrophe of unprecedented proportions.

He was a body of warm and translucent water on which two land masses floated. Submarine currents whispered to his bones and neurons, commingled, and spawned marvellous chimera. To all observers, Fernando was a boy like any other at Crestview Public School: he played road hockey, he laughed, he raced his bike, but a spectroscope (or similar pataphysical device) would have revealed two hearts, two tongues, two memories. Fernando was in deep cover. Accepting Canadian citizenship, he believed, would mean relinquishing forever the possibility of travelling freely between those contingent worlds whose existence he sensed and enwrapped.

No alphabet existed to phrase what he felt. His sentiments might have been expressed as a piece of music, a concerto perhaps, for *charango*, cello, and radio telescope. It would have been a marvellous and harrowing music: music for exiles, refugees, and rocket ships lost forever in space; nostalgic, tentative, bloody, epic and fractional at once. The concerto might enfold a song, an elegy, sung or intoned by a boy soprano, to which the only words that could be understood were: Nona, Nona, Nona.

His mother would never accept his quasi-mystical feelings as an explanation or defence of his decision not to become a Canadian citizen. He was angry. Why should he have to explain? It was the way he felt. It was what he wanted. There was no need for anything to change.

Disconsolate and uncomfortable, he wriggled out of the tube. Preoccupied as he was, he put a foot wrong on the lip of the tube and fell, driving his nose into the wooden post before his hands were even free of the pockets of his jacket. The fierce pain and sudden hot splash of blood on his lips frightened him and he almost cried. One hand on the post and the other on the wooden platform of the playground equipment, blood streaming over his lips, Fernando's small body shook with two sharp sobs. He was miserably alone. And it was all his fault. Everything. The bloody nose, the citizenship. He wiped his lips, sat down, put his head back and looked into the washed out sky.

He put a hand to his nostrils. He considered blood. The blood of Christ that they drank in the Mass. His mother said it was only wine but Catholics believed it was transubstantiated, transformed, just like the bread they ate was really the Body of Christ. It was both things at once: particle and wave, wine and blood. He thought about the blood sacrifices of the Aztecs and the blood spilled by the conquistadors all over New Spain. He thought about the blood that he shared with his family, his ancestors. He wondered if his blood might be different from other blood, say Michael Redmond's blood, in some way that could not be measured yet.

(Years later, while preparing sauce for a lasagne he intended to serve to his mother, his nose would begin to bleed spontaneously and he would recall not this nose bleed in the playground, but the earlier sanguineous incident with Michael Redmond.)

Seven years old, Michael and Fernando had made their way home through chest deep snow and wondered aloud what their mothers had in mind for dinner.

"Sloppy Joes probably."

Oh wondrous Sloppiness of the Joe! Fernando thought. Never having eaten one, never having sighted one, he imagined meat of such tenderness it deliquesced as the shadow of a fork passed over it; seasoned to perfection with salt, oregano and pepper; a few sautéed onions perhaps; fresh tomato; a flash of green parsley. He longed for one with the terrible desire of a seven-year-old. O Joe! O Sloppy!

Fernando said that maybe they'd have lasagne at his house. He had no idea what they would be eating—more likely they'd be eating loathsome *hígado* or the reviled *pastel de pescado*—but lasagne was the only food he could conceive of that might aspire to the delectable status of The Sloppy Joe. Michael expressed his enthusiasm for lasagne and urged Fernando to describe how his mother made it.

"Noodles."

"Right."

"Tomato sauce."

"Right."

"Ground beef."

"What?"

"Ground beef," Fernando repeated

"Hamburger you mean?" asked Michael.

"Yeah, meat for hamburgers."

"Yeah, right."

"Cheese."

"What kind?"

"Mozzarella and parmesan."

"Huh?"

"Two kinds," Fernando explained, "mozzarella on the inside and parmesan on the very top."

Michael disagreed. "My mum puts cottage cheese in it."

Canadian cuisine, in Fernando's opinion, ran from the sublime, such as Sloppy Joes, to the obscene, such as cottage cheese. "Ugh. Gross."

"No it's not."

"Yes it is."

"No it's not." Michael gave Fernando a shove which Fernando returned, insisting all the while that cottage cheese was gross and had no place in lasagne. Michael refused to back down.

"What would you know about it?" Fernando finally asked. "You eat Chef Boyardee."

"So?" The shove accompanying that monosyllable sent Fernando flying bum-first into the snow. He lay there glaring at Michael.

"So Chef Boyardee is garbage. What would you know about real Italian food?"

"What would you know?"

"A lot more than you. I know you don't put stinky cottage cheese in lasagne."

Fernando was about to authenticate his lasagne by reference to his grandfather's emigration from Italy when Michael jumped on him, threw snow down his back, rubbed it in his face and yelled, "Shut up shut up eat some cottage cheese." Fernando struggled to get up, a struggle exacerbated by the layers of bulky winter clothing he wore, and inadvertently drove his face into Michael's knee. Both boys heard and felt the thunk as proboscis met kneecap. There was a brief silence, then a fierce wailing as the snow turned a deep, sickening, pink.

Twelve years later in his cramped kitchen, Fernando will remember all this as blood drips onto the cutting board. When he presents the lasagne to his mother she will smile approvingly until he serves her a portion and she espies what she believes to be cottage cheese.

"*Tiene* cottage cheese?"

"No," Fernando will reply, tersely flinging an Italian cookbook onto the table, "ricotta. Ricotta.")

Fernando watched the birds, black specks circling high above him. His nose had stopped bleeding, though it still throbbed with pain. It was late and he had resolved nothing, decided on nothing. He took some comfort in the knowledge that, in the world of sub-atomic physics, from a quantum perspective, all possible outcomes of a situation exist side by side until the situation is observed. He hoped he hadn't been observed. He made his way home for supper.

The clink of forks on plates, murmurs of appreciation and fragments of conversation camouflaged the deeper silence which underscored their meals together. Lina set her fork down and sought with her tongue a small piece of meat that had burrowed between two teeth. She noticed something different about her son's face. His eyes looked puffy. As if he'd been crying. Fernando was certain she was going to ask him what he had decided, and chose that moment to mention that he'd found a good telescope, not too expensive, in the catalogue. Octavio said he'd take a look at it later. Lina decided the boy was fine, maybe a little tired, perhaps in need of a vitamin supplement.

The following day, Thursday, Fernando Suárez settled on a desperate course of action as a way out of his impending, unwanted transmutation into a Canadian. He would become the anti-citizen. He decided to break the law and get caught.

Shoplifting seemed the simplest solution. He resolved not to think about how, where, or what he would steal; he would simply give himself over to the forces of chance and inspiration. Across the street from his school, where he caught the bus to take him home, was Lincoln Plaza, a small mall with a grocery store which opened on one side to a drug store which also had a separate entrance, a dry cleaner, a pizza outlet, a beauty salon (Beauty Beyond), an ill-lighted insurance office, and a pet food store.

He walked into the busy grocery store and wandered the aisles waiting for something to claim his attention. Cans of beans; cans of peas; cans of corn; cans of soup: vegetable, beef noodle, chicken noodle, chicken with rice, mushroom; cans of spaghetti with tomato sauce. He shuddered. Canadians liked food in cans: another reason he couldn't be Canadian.

Fernando realized he had lost track of why he had come into the store in the first place. Steal something. He looked around again. Steal what? Macaroni loaf? No thanks. Garlic Coil sausage? A tub of baby beef liver? No, this wouldn't do. He couldn't steal anything here. He decided to try the drug store and see if anything there exerted a magnetic influence.

Having resolved to steal something from the drug store, he immediately felt obscenely nervous. Hideously warm in his windbreaker, he felt sick and dizzy. He thought he might need to be hospitalized. He believed he might faint. He thought his heart might stop. He didn't want to die. He just wanted to steal something and get caught so that he wouldn't be granted his citizenship because he wasn't a good citizen. That's all. He stood in an aisle filled with Tampax and pads and other mysterious, embarrassing items. Personal lubricant. Ohmigod.

It wasn't working. He couldn't steal a box of Tampax. They'd think he was a pervert. He'd probably have to see a psychiatrist and maybe be given electroshock therapy and it would all end up on his Permanent Record and he'd never get into a good university and never become an obscure but important physicist. No, spontaneity wasn't working for him. He needed to plan. He left the store.

He sat on the cold, wet (it had rained briefly earlier) curb, and tried to think. Dead leaves of newspaper curled at his feet. Steal something. Make it obvious so you get caught. Get the police involved, make sure they call your parents, well, your mum. And then? He had read something in the newspaper about the crime rate involving refugees. There were a lot of people who wanted to deport refugees who committed crimes. Could they deport him? He wasn't a refugee. He didn't want to be deported. All he wanted was to stay in Canada as a Landed Immigrant, as an Outsider.

No, he wouldn't be deported he decided. He was a minor and they wouldn't deport his entire family simply because he'd stolen a comic book. There. He'd decided. A comic book. Good. Easy Peasy Japanesey. He marched back into the drug store through the front door, the same door he'd exited through only minutes ago. That was bound to look suspicious. Good. That's what he wanted.

Fernando Suárez, thirteen years old, heart rate 91 b.p.m., eyes flitting psychotically from side to side, hands stuffed in his pockets and excruciatingly aware of the space behind his back, stumbled toward the magazine rack. He undid his jacket. He couldn't see any comic books. There were dozens of magazines for ladies: Chatelaine and Redbook and Women's Week and fashion magazines and there were car magazines and sports magazines and and—

He glanced quickly around and reached up, on his toes, to the last row on the shelves. He pulled down one of the thick, glossy magazines. It fairly burned his hands. Fernando Suárez, thirteen, heart rate 100 b.p.m., temperature thirty-seven point nine and climbing, bowed his head and listened intently for footsteps, voices. He flipped the pages toward the middle of the magazine.

There were so many photographs he didn't know where to look first. Her name was Cindi May and she was only six years older than Fernando. What a difference a few years could make. Where did girls like her come from? She was from Missouri and she liked dancing and skinny dipping. Fernando didn't like either of those activities but he sure liked Cindi May. In the centrefold picture she appeared completely naked except for a pair of blue and white cowboy boots, a white cowboy hat and a long blue scarf which she held tightly across her body and through which he could make out her marvellous breasts. She smiled a happy smile.

A man's voice in the next aisle startled him and he hastily replaced the magazine before remembering that he had planned to steal something and had just missed a perfect opportunity to do so. He turned to the rotating display tower beside the shelves of magazines and discovered the comic books. They looked cheap and dull after the glossy, full colour reproductions in the magazine. He chose a comic book called *Tales of Gore*. It had two stories in it, narrated by a decomposing zombie named Creepy Pete. The first was a war story about a soldier who went insane in the trenches and eviscerated the other soldiers in his unit. The crazy soldier finally died because he choked on a piece of gristle in the mess. Fernando found it hard to concentrate on the comic book. His thoughts kept returning to Cindi May and her blue scarf. The second story was about a bear that attacked an isolated farming community. Fernando returned the comic book to its place.

Time had become wildly elastic. Night might have fallen. For all he knew the store had closed already and he was locked inside, forgotten. He turned back to the magazine rack and reached up again to take the first magazine. He got hold of it and held it tightly in his hands. He stared at the cover. Cindi May was on the cover too; she looked kind of angry in her bathing suit, but in a nice way. He sucked in his stomach and pushed the magazine half way into his pants then zipped up his jacket to cover it up. He moved away from the magazine rack with some difficulty. He remembered that he wanted to be caught so he tried to undo his jacket zipper but now it seemed to be stuck. He walked directly in front of the checkout, looking right at the clerk. His entire demeanour, he was sure, screamed out: I AM A THIEF. I AM THE ANTI-CITIZEN. ARREST ME. There was an infinite distance to traverse before reaching the front door. He shoulder ached with the expectation of a restraining hand. His hand went to the door. He pushed. Stepped outside. They were just waiting for him to leave the premises. That was the way they did it. Then they nabbed you. He was half way across the parking lot. He had achieved escape velocity. He was almost on the bus. He was almost at home. He was beyond the event horizon. It was almost Friday; he was almost a citizen. He had not been caught.

Fernando Suárez, saddest boy in the country, heart rate barely discernible, stood outside the door to Fred's Drugs staring at the ground. The concrete was littered with dead matches, crushed cigarette butts, dirty gum wrappers. He walked into the store for the third time in ten minutes, went to the cashier, put the magazine on the counter and said, "I stole this."

"You stole this?" The clerk was black. Incredibly, Fernando had not noticed this detail earlier. He was probably the only black person in the whole city. How could he not have noticed?

"Yes."

"I see." He had a beautiful voice, like music. Winston, the clerk with the beautiful voice, looked at the cover of the magazine then Fernando's face and looked at the magazine again. He wasn't entirely certain what to do next. "When?"

"When did I steal it? Just now."

"Under my nose? Just like that?"

"Yeah."

"Well...It's good you brought it back." Winston turned the magazine over, his fine fingers tracing vague circles on the cigarette advertisement on the back cover, then finally put the magazine under the counter and said, "I hope you learned your lesson."

Fernando waited. Winston waited. At the back of the store, the pharmacist sang *Lucy In The Sky With Diamonds* while organizing the vitamins. Finally, Fernando asked, "Aren't you going to call my parents? The cops?"

"I don't think so. I don't see any need." Winston was torn between wanting to just talk to the boy and feeling that he had an official duty to discharge as an employee and representative of Fred's Drugs. He was about to say something about how he thought those magazines should be kept elsewhere but instead said, "Let's just make sure it's the last time."

Fernando was exhausted. He needed chocolate, a coke, a nap. "Where are you from?" he asked the clerk.

"What difference does that make?"

"Are you a Canadian citizen?"

"Hey what is this, boy? What are you getting at?"

"Don't get mad. I'm not a Canadian citizen."

"You're not?"

"You have a nice voice."

"I have a nice voice. Man, what is this?"

"It's not anything. I just wondered if you were from somewhere else. Like me."

Winston regarded Fernando with some suspicion. "I'm from Trinidad." The boy didn't say anything. Winston's face softened. "You know where that is?"

"Sort of. In the Caribbean?"

"That's right," Winston nodded. Fernando smiled. "Where you from?" Fernando told him. "Is that right? Well, you listen...what's your name, anyway?"

"Fernando."

"Fernando. That's a cool name. Listen, Fernando, you and I are like neighbours, right? We are from the same part of the world, you understand. We share a past, a patrimony. Well, not exactly, but we share a difference right? We're different from everybody else. We have to look out for one another. You understand? There's a lot of people don't care too much for people like me and you. Yes? So we have to watch out for each other. I won't turn you in for making this mistake. And next time you should think about trying to steal from your brother." Even as he said all this, Winston thought he could have explained it better and wondered what the boy would make of it.

Fernando found himself apologizing.

"People make mistakes. It was good you brought it back." A couple approached the counter and asked if the store carried birthday cards. Winston indicated the appropriate aisle.

"What's your name?"

"Me? I'm Winston."

"Winston. Do you work here all the time?"

"Part-time. I go to school."

"Where?"

"The university."

"Oh yeah? My dad teaches there. Math. What are you studying?"

"Political science."

"I want to be a scientist. A physicist."

"Is that right?"

"Yeah."

The couple left without buying a card. Fernando thought the cards at Fred's were ugly; they probably did too.

"Are you a Canadian citizen?"

"Uh uh, no. Why do you keep asking?"

"Are you going to be?"

"Canadian? No thank you. I'm going back to Trinidad in a few years. I hope."

"Yeah?"

"I'm not staying here. No."

"What's Trinidad like?"

"Boy, Trinidad is mas." He laughed. Fernando smiled at Winston; he liked the way Winston laughed. "Oh man, Fernando, I got to get to work you know, put this shit away. This stuff, I mean." He kicked a cardboard box lightly with the toe of his running shoe and smiled some more.

"Okay."

"Okay Fernando, stay cool."

"Can I just ask you something? Should I become a Canadian? I'm a landed immigrant. My parents are getting their citizenship and they want to know if I want mine too."

"Fernando, I don't know, man. I don't know anything about you. You know what you need to do. You know who you are. Be true to yourself. Whatever it takes."

That hadn't worked out the way he had envisioned, but he had met Winston. Winston was cool. And smart. That was a rare combination. Winston seemed to be cool without even trying. He was cool even in his white Fred's Drugs jacket. Maybe that was something that happened if you were from Trinidad or maybe it was because he was older. Winston was probably about the same age as Cindi May. He thought about that for a moment. It was an exciting image. All that smooth skin, Winston's the colour of coffee, and Cindi May's like honey. And Winston's smooth voice that was like a song when he spoke, rising and falling like gentle waves.

"Whatever it takes," he had said.

Fernando suddenly found sitting on the bus uncomfortable. He hoped the source of his discomfort didn't show. Fernando often laboured under the misapprehension that everyone watched him and could see his gaffes, hesitations, and unbidden erections. No one looked at Fernando; no one noticed him at all.

As the bus rattled away from Winston and closer to Fernando's home, the now familiar anguish descended on him again. He passed row upon row of indistinguishable row houses. His thoughts turned to crime again. He needed to do something too dramatic to be missed. Blow something up, rob a bank, hijack a bus....

***

The glass, chipped in one corner and stressed by an incorrectly installed display case, had been cracked last week by a stone shot like a bullet from under the tire of car spinning donuts in the empty parking lot. Mike had noticed the crack in the morning, had put in a phone call to head office and written up an incident report about it but nothing had been done. When Fernando threw himself and the rock in his hands against it, the pane sheared along the crack and gave way from the fissured corner. The glass swung down sharp as a sword and much heavier, cutting through Fernando's jacket and skin and then broke into several treacherous looking pieces at his feet.

***

"Why are you calling me at home?" Even though she was alone, answering the phone to hear Mike's voice had profoundly shocked Lina.

"It's an emergency."

"What?"

"It's Fernando. Your son, Fernando. He smashed into the window of the store. He smashed it with a rock. It broke. A huge piece of it broke off. He's all right I think. He's cut. He's bleeding. Not too bad. I've called for an ambulance. They're on their way. He's conscious. I think you should come right away. Lina?"

An image of Fernando bisected by an enormous pane of glass and lying in a pool of sticky red blood immobilized her.

"Lina?"

"I'm on my way."

While the doctor at the emergency ward stitched up Fernando's arm, Lina tried repeatedly to call her husband. There was no answer at his office and she eventually left a message with the receptionist. Lina knew where he was but couldn't think about it now. Her mind was full of Fernando. He had been lucky. His left arm (such thin arms, like sticks, he'd always been thin) needed a dozen stitches but there were no other consequences.

Fernando emerged from the doctor's care, pale and fragile. She pressed him to her, mindful of his arm. She hugged him to her bosom like he was a little boy and kissed the top of his head passionately. He was a little boy. She held his face in her hands and looked into his eyes, murmuring, "*Ai, mijo, mijito, mi amor.*"

"I'm okay Mama. I'm okay."

Her eyes filled with tears and she hugged him again. "*Ai Fernando, Panchito, qué pasó, qué pasó?*"

"It was an accident mama. I fell."

"*Ai Dios Mio.*" She crushed him against her again. In the back of the taxi home she smoked and held him close and stroked his hair and kissed him and cried. Fernando was miserable but tried not to let it show so his mother wouldn't worry. He had failed. Everything had gone wrong. He had lost.

***

A traveller entering a black hole would be dragged around the hole as it rotated. One moment everything would be unimaginably bright and the next, utterly dark. The traveller would move at increasingly greater, unbelievable, speeds. His feet would weigh about a trillion times as much as his head. Sucked further down the black hole (Fernando pictured the drain in the kitchen sink magnified a million billion times and making a sucking sound so loud and hideous it was inconceivable), the traveller's body would disintegrate into its constituent atoms and then, smashing into the core of the black hole, an area of infinite density and infinite gravity called the singularity, he would be absolutely, entirely, crushed out of existence.

It was well past midnight. Downstairs, his parents fought. They had been fighting off and on for hours. They had started talking calmly, rationally, after Fernando had gone to bed but now they talked over each other, raising their voices to make their points. They yelled, hissed, and accused, switching from Spanish to English and back to Spanish effortlessly. Had Fernando seen them he would have been shocked by the ugliness and force of their expressions. His father made uncharacteristic faces of disgust and mockery, his carefully combed hair unravelling with each toss and shake, while his mother made violent and accusatory gestures with her small hands, the polish on her nails flashing angrily. But he could only imagine what they looked like from the invective they hurled at one another. The air around him raged with the explosions of their anger and resentment and Fernando could not close his eyes.

Early Friday morning, Judge Nicholas Jones-Ross granted Canadian citizenship to Octavio Garcia Suárez, Lina Isabel Suárez, and, in absentia, to Fernando Juan Garcia Suárez. Afterwards, Lina stood in the bureaucratic hallway and cried quietly, creating an eddy in the traffic of men and women hurrying to their various meetings, hearings, and appointments. Octavio tried to put his arm around her but she threw it off and walked away, found a taxi and left.

Fernando awoke late in his darkened room with a faint headache and an itching in his arm. He raised the blind on the window, then sat back down on the bed to wait for his eyes to adjust to the brilliance of the daylight. He considered his arm disinterestedly, noted the stitches extruding from the skin and remembered: the crashing glass; his mother, diminished and worried in the waiting room; the fight and the raging, wounded voices last night. He half-hoped to hear his father clanging about in the basement or his mother moving about, vacuuming the dining room, but he heard nothing. The house was empty and soundless. Outside, the world held its breath, reserved judgement, told him nothing.

He sat on his bed. He did not count the boats on the bed spread nor did his unfocused eyes note the drifting dust motes. He did not discern patterns in the orange-brown carpet. He could not hear his blood nor perceive his lungs' systole. He sat, still and small, hands patiently folded in his lap, and waited for the countless billion atoms of his body to scatter into the primordial maw of the universe.

Somewhere, doors closed swiftly and conclusively. Paths through dense ethereal forests, tracks across marvellous adamantine desert floors, vanished, leaving no traces for navigators and pilgrims. Trade winds ceased. Maps disintegrated. Fernando, or a feral consciousness now animate within him, sensed a kind of death in the air and began to howl with grief for the withering away of a world he only now was certain had ever existed.

Letter From Tucuman

The moon is very bright. From my window seat, I can make out the shapes of the landscape. A dry countryside: long grasses, short, gnarled, intense trees. Old man trees. Soft, round hills. In the middle of absolutely nowhere stands a handful of shacks. Some have electric lights and TV antennae. There is one shack with only three walls (like a proscenium theatre: I think of you.) A bonfire burns in the centre of the stage and a figure squats beside the flames. Weird, distorted shadows play on the back wall.

I wake up in the brilliant, almost painful, morning light. We are very high up. Are these mountains? Rock and snow reflect silver light everywhere. We negotiate tight curves, descending. The bus juts out over the edge of the road as we turn, leans out into nothing, air, emptiness, a plunge of I don't know how many deadly metres. Suddenly, impossibly quickly, the rock becomes red earth; there is green and water. We have crossed something, a line, a barrier, a season. It seems that we are descending into spring although spring is still weeks away.

All night I thought about all the things that have gone wrong in my life. This morning, the list has grown. First, there is Mom and Dad. (Of course.) My parents who never did anything to me, who were very good to me, supportive, helpful, loving. My parents that I never trusted, never knew. I remember feeling afraid, this is when I was grown, a man I mean, afraid that I would be alone with my father in their house. Not afraid that he would hurt me or anything, just afraid that we would be alone together and would have to talk to each other and what would we ever say? No doubt he was equally worried. How stupid. What was there to be afraid of?

Then, there is the divorce which still gives me grief. I thought I had dealt with all that. Mourned and worked through it, but quite probably I worked through nothing, I just felt lousy for a while. It's guilt I suppose. Failure. It occurred to me that I have never completed anything in my life. I am forever leaving. I left high school. I left college. I left all my crummy jobs without ever giving notice. I left my marriage. Now, I've left the country (albeit temporarily.)

From here, it is a short distance to admit that most of my friendships have been failures. That I am not good with intimacy, not good at trusting, at needing (my ex-wife used to tell me that), that I am terrified of failing, of appearing weak. I am unable to love men in their gladness. I cannot rejoice in my friends' successes. I am envious, spiteful. I have no moral centre, no real beliefs to sustain me. (I make my living by taking photographs of shoes, for crissake.) I cannot line dance. Let's admit it: I am a wreck, a hopeless, pathetic, textbook case.

The bus stops. In the middle of nothing. We are all asked to get out and proceed to the little shack off the side of the road. Have we crossed a border? Not that I know of. (Perhaps I'm on the wrong bus. "Excuse me, is this the bus to Pebble Beach?") But here are a bunch of soldiers looking very bored in rumpled uniforms checking our passports and chain smoking cigarettes. No explanation is offered. Nothing exciting happens; no questions are asked. We all troop back onto the bus.

I decide, as we descend farther into the green land, that I will change my life. I am going to take charge of my life. I am going to get healthy. Mentally and physically. I will quit smoking. When I get back to Canada. I will jog. No I won't; I hate jogging. I will walk everywhere. I won't do that either. Ride a bike, yes. That's what I'll do. I'll buy a bike and ride it everywhere. Save on parking, build up some muscle in my legs, look good in shorts. I'll join a gym even. Sure.

Also: I will find a therapist. Why not? I'm forever telling my friends they should go see somebody; why the hell don't I? I need it more than they do. I am going to get help. Hi, I'm a fuck-up and I need help. There. I said it. I am going to get my shit together. I am.

Then, when I am healthy and together and have great leg muscles from cycling everywhere and a fabulous butt (they have machines, you know, in those gyms, give you a butt like a green apple) and get the tobacco stains off my teeth, I will seek you out and steal you away from that stockbroker or crane salesman or whatever he is that you live with. No, I won't. I don't know what I'll do about you. I will forget you. I will.

Yes, I am going to get well and live the rest of my life.

This is a tired, broken-down city crowded with bicycles, cars, trucks, buses, women with large bags and men in suits. There are signs everywhere: boil your water; avoid diarrhoea; wash your hands; keep your city clean.

When I get off the bus, a dozen men appear offering taxis, hotels, and assistance for the weary traveller. I let someone carry my bags and take me to a hotel. The hotel, he assures me, is reasonable, has a family environment. Whatever that means. We climb into his car. I've never seen a car quite like this. I mean I've seen cars like it, it's a small Fiat, but inside it's gutted. There's no upholstery, no dash board, no windows. It looks like a bomb wreck. I consider, for a moment, the possibility that he is going to drive me into the middle of a cane field and murder me. I've climbed into a stranger's car, put my bags in his trunk and I have no idea where we're going. We drive. He talks non-stop: weather report, history lesson, political analysis: This country will never get ahead. Change the attitude of the boss, change the attitude of the worker, very difficult. It's corrupt from the top down to the lowest guy on the ladder. Change that. Very difficult.

The way he says 'this country' with such regret.

He asks me where I come from. I tell him: Canada. Ah, he says. They know how to work there, he says. I tell him that they seem to know how to work here too and he laughs. He asks me where I've been. I tell him. He asks me, and maybe I misunderstand him, if I had seen any people on my bus with a certain kind of doll about this big, so tall, indicating with his hands. I say, no, I didn't see any dolls. Ah, says he. Why? I finally ask. He tells me that it's his daughter's birthday tomorrow and she would like one of these dolls very much and he thought maybe he'd go back to the bus station and see if anybody had one to sell but if no one brought any in then there's no point. I guess these particular dolls aren't available in this city then. Black market dolls available only in the capital or across the border perhaps. Or I misunderstand him entirely.

We arrive at the hotel. (He hasn't murdered me in a cane field after all, you see.) It looks very reasonable. Kind of place you might bring a family. (That's what family environment means.) He takes my bags out of the trunk and runs them up to my room while I check in. I pay him and he tells me that if I want to see a bit of the city, if I want a bit of a tour he'd be glad to take me around. I tell him that yes, maybe later I'll take a bit of a tour.

Hours later, I've unpacked, showered and dressed for the evening. I am on my way out in search of a drink before dinner. He sits behind the front desk watching the TV. His eyes are soft, out of focus, and he looks tired in the blue television light. He notices me in his peripheral vision and, with effort, like a big dog rousing itself out of sleep in the sun, pulls himself back into this world. He asks, smiling now, his dark eyes sharp again, if maybe I'd like to go for that tour. I tell him: not tonight, I'm tired and a bit hungry, I just want to get a bite to eat and make it an early night but maybe another day. He looks terribly disappointed, then shrugs and slowly returns to the television.

All night long I can't get his face out of my mind. It sits there like The Great Toad of Misery: round, fallen, sagging. I see his face and imagine the doll he was asking about for his daughter whose birthday is tomorrow. (That rare doll available only to those who have made the treacherous bus trip to the capital or farther.) I imagine a doll that looks nothing like the inhabitants of this place and yet is considered by all the city's five-year-old girls to be the apogee of beauty. The doll has blond hair and blue eyes and a pink dress and makes a mewing noise if you turn her upside down and wets herself after you give her a bottle. I understand that he needs the money he would have made from taking me on a tour tonight to buy a present for his daughter.

My earlier enthusiasm for therapy and happiness and a good life disintegrates. What, what the hell would I ever say to a therapist?

I am monumentally sad. Feel here, Dr. Therapist, in the centre of my chest. You see, it sinks in, it gives way where there should be solid bone. No, I have only a softness, a fading, a dull pressure collapsing inward. I am down, Dr. Therapist. I am depressed, incapacitated, by all the sadness ever: the lonely dead no one ever mourned; the hundreds of thousands of lost souls, hurled into salty darkness in the bottom of a man-made lake or a cold stinking cell. I am sad for all whose turn will never come, those who wait and wait and wait. I am sad, Dr. Therapist, for all the misery and all the poor. I am sad for all the vicious cruelty unleashed on tender flesh, Dr. Therapist. I am sad for the bored soldiers in their rumpled uniforms. I am sad for the guy who found me at the bus terminal and asked about a doll for his daughter whose birthday is tomorrow. And yes, I'm even sad for Old Yeller and every other scrap of sentimental horseshit ever invented. I am sad over this stupid life and sad too that we must leave it, and I want to weep and dump ashes on my head, Dr. Therapist, but I'm afraid if I start crying I'll never stop. I am profoundly sad because the one I want does not want me. So tell me, tell me please, you who have studied the secrets of dreams and the mind and the spirit, tell me, Dr. Therapist, what to do.

How would I ever say that?

Money In The Bank

"Have an audition for you Federico Wednesday 2:15 movie of the week that D.D Howden is casting called *Breaking Trust* they want to see you for the part of Pincho, a motor-mouthed Cuban or whatever. (Inhalation) Pincho is in his late 20s early 30s he's not good-looking but doesn't know it script is in the office call to confirm thanks byebye."

I'm an actor. A legitimate actor. I've trained. I've studied Stanislavsky, Feldenkreis, Alexander, Grotowski, Meisner and Lecoq. I understand sense-memory and super-objectives. I know about emotional recall, the swamp, alignment and units. I am intimate with soft palates and glottal shock. I comprehend iambic pentameter and shared lines; stillness and contra-mask; diphthongs and schwas; blank verse, stage fighting, hitting a mark, bananas, half-apples and looping. I even know a thing or two about acting.

I'm a good actor and I work, mostly, in the theatre. I make my living from it; it's not a hobby. Yes, you may have seen me on television. From time to time, I sell my skills in exchange for easy money. You've probably seen me in some small role in a banal television show or movie. I played, for example, the librarian (Librarian: Microfiche? Up the stairs to your left.) in *Forever Murder*. *Forever Murder,* you remember, that's the one about the guy who gets killed and it turns out the other guy did it. I also played Eddy the sniper in *Deadly Suspicion*. That's the one where the guy gets killed and then the other guy dies and it turns out that the third guy did it. You get the idea. I've also played priests, lawyers, policemen, a marine biologist, four waiters (two French, two plain), and an assortment of criminals.

This thing, this M.O.W. (movie of the week), *Breaking Trust*, is an F.P.G. (flaming piece of garbage). It's about a doctor who worked for a few years in Latin America and he's come back now to North America, a haunted man. A troubled man. The doctor's name is Chad Boswell and, here I'm quoting, "he looks tough as nails with a face as worn as leather, till you look into his eyes. Eyes that look on with the Sadness of the Ages. Eyes that have seen more than most. Seen and remembered. Everything. The enormous Sadness of his eyes is belied only by the inexorability of his jaw." He's so goddamn sad it has to be capitalized. Seems he got up to all sorts of things while he was in Latin America including selling one of his kidneys for money to buy medicine. He works with the police now, as a special advisor, which gives "some meaning to his life" but he's "barely holding on."

This Pincho character I'm auditioning for overhears a suspicious conversation and comes to Chad, who is "a familiar figure in the barrio," and tells him, "Man, I seen and hear a lotta weird things growing up in the barrio, but nothing as weird as this."

It ain't Chekhov, man.

The auditions for *Breaking Trust* (what does that title mean?) are being held, for some obscure reason, in the offices of a modeling agency. I walk in, glance around, nod to one or two actors I recognize from other auditions and head for the receptionist. She is speaking into one of those tiny headset phones. She looks airbrushed, as if she's stepped off the cover of a fashion magazine. She has killer-bee-stung lips, orthodontically corrected, dazzling teeth, and terrible diction.

"Who'zit wanna speak to?"

"Okay. And whomaysay is calling?"

"Uh huh. Venus, okay." The person on the other end of the phone is clearly named Venus.

"And wha's regarding Venus?"

"Uh huh, okay."

I tell her I'm here to audition for *Breaking Trust*. She smiles her orthodontically perfect smile and tells me that they're a little behind schedule and just have a seat. When I'm called in, I give my picture and resume to D.D. Howden, the casting director, and greet the producers, a bored looking man and a woman and the director, a squat fellow with thin lips and a tanned head.

D.D. asks if I have any questions before we start and I say, "Yes, do you want an accent?"

The director seems confused. "Accent?"

I explain, "Well, he's referred to as a Cuban, I thought he might have a Cuban accent."

The director takes a moment to bring his full attention to this question. He looks over at the producers then turns back to me and asks, "What accent are you doing?"

"I'm not doing an accent."

D.D. jumps in to clarify, "He detects an accent." Oh does he? The director asks again, "What accent is that you've got?"

"A Canadian accent?"

There is silence. Then the director, whose eyes are too close together, stretches his thin lips into a smile, rolls his too-close-together eyes in the direction of the producers

85

and, still smiling, as if agreeing to play along with my excellent joke, asks, "And where would this Canadian accent come from?" He lays special stress on the word Canadian to show me he knows I'm being silly.

"It would be from southwestern Ontario. Do you know where that is?"

The piggy, little, bald director chuckles. The producers do not. The corpulent, bearded man looks at the carpeting and the woman whose face reminds me of a nail looks out the window. Neither of them offer an opinion on my accent.

"A Canadian accent," he says again.

That's right you sun-scorched moron, a Canadian accent. If it wasn't for my name you wouldn't imagine any accent because I speak English as well as you do. In fact, I speak it better than you do. Because I've been to theatre school and I have good diction. I like finishing my words; I pay attention to endings. I can spray spittle for metres should the necessity arise. I can sound all the consonants in the word facts. Not only do I sound them but I conjoin them into an elegant whole, much the same way a good pianist plays a run of 32nd notes.

The director's accent originates, I would guess, at a railway crossing just outside Rochester, New York, which, it is well known, is one of the elocution capitals of the world and home to one of the most pleasing English accents on the planet. On top of his Rochester rail yard accent, he has the West Coast vowel sag that comes with fifteen years of living in Los Angeles.

Suddenly intense, getting down to the solemn business of casting a TV movie, he growls, "Do a Cuban accent. Can you do a Cuban accent?"

"Cuban. Certainly."

I give him a Panamanian accent. He does not mention the sixteen hundred kilometre discrepancy. When the audition is over, I race out of the modeling agency and throw the script into the nearest garbage can I can find.

I get the job. They want me for two days which means (with overtime) that I don't have to worry about rent for two months. Money in the bank.

There have been some revisions since my audition. Pincho is now called Cook. That's what he does. He's a cook, hence the name. Cook and Wife, his wife, run a greasy spoon. They are also, it seems, sheltering a young El Salvadoran woman and her family.

In the scene we're shooting today, I have one line: "The washroom is downstairs." I practice the line, giving it Tex-Mex, Chilango, Cuban and Andalusian flavourings. I also practice it "angry," "happy" and "in the throes of an existential crisis." I put on my cook's outfit and head to Make-up. Where they paint me brown. I can't quite believe it's happening, but sure enough, that's my face in the mirror and it is going brown. I have nothing against brown, but if they wanted brown they could have hired a brown actor, no? I ask Make-up why she's going so dark with the base and she says, "You're the Cook aren't you? The Latino Cook?"

"Yes."

"And Alejandra," she says, "your wife, she's dark too."

Right. I watch her in the mirror, a peroxide blonde with wide, bloodshot eyes. She smiles as she browns out my hands. *Who is that masked man? This is brown face. This is a minstrel show. And I'm the Cook, aren't I? The Latino Cook. I hope no one sees this.*

This business of being brown confuses me. I feel somehow that it is wrong but I can't quite put my finger on what it is about it that disturbs me. *It's only make-up. It's just acting.* It doesn't mean anything. Feeling a little vulnerable, I walk quickly to my trailer where I can hide and maybe knock off a few more chapters of *Jude the Obscure*, but on the way, I'm waylaid by an actor I know.

Mark wants to talk about the "State of the Industry." He's worked up about the number of American productions currently shooting in town that use Canadian actors only in small roles. "All the leads are cast out of L.A.," he hisses.

"All of them?"

"Yeah. They might read a few Canadians to make it look good but everything ends up going to the Americans. You know what they call us?"

"Hmmm?"

"Ice-niggers."

"What?"

"That's what they call us. Ice-niggers."

"Who calls us that?"

"The Americans."

"Ice-niggers? That's outrageous. You've heard that?"

"Ice-niggers."

Mark says nothing about my make-up.

Over the next few hours, I am visited sporadically by Axel, the third A.D., who stops by to see how I'm doing, what I'm reading, ("Oh yeah.") and to tell me that we won't get to my scene before dinner. Axel says nothing about my make-up.

Over dinner, a delightful, Cajun-type chicken thing with lemongrass and rice, I meet Alejandra who plays Wife, and Gloria who plays Rosa, the illegal alien. Alejandra is round and soft like a gnocchi. Gloria is equally small but thin, all sharp angles. Neither one says anything about my make-up.

"I almost saw you in a play," Gloria tells me.

"Almost?"

"We were all ready to go but at the last minute I got scared."

"Scared?"

"I just couldn't go. I felt afraid. I didn't want to leave the children."

I finish my mousse and try to imagine what she might be afraid of.

"It wasn't rational. Mario, my husband kept telling me, 'Let's go, it's all right, this is Canada' and I knew it was something, a feeling from El Salvador, but I just couldn't go. Fear." She smiles as she says this.

Days later, Andrea, my agent, phones to tell me that *Breaking Trust* has hired a young boy who doesn't speak any English and the production office wants to know if I'd be willing to come in again to work as a translator. Ordinarily, I would never agree to this kind of thing; it doesn't look very professional to be doing extra, odd jobs on set. But today, I'm distracted by laughter outside my window, and it seems like easy money so, "Sure. Why not?"

Monday morning, early, I report to the location: the Coroner's Building. It hadn't registered before but the Coroner's Building is the morgue. I imagined a lot of clean offices and a few equally clean coroners. I hadn't factored in the dead bodies. They're actually bringing one in as I roam around looking for an assistant director.

I find Axel, who's watching them unload the corpse and tell him I'm here to translate for the kid. "Great," he says. "Lenin's in Make-up."

"Who? What's his name?"

"Lenin."

"His name's Lenin? The kid is named Lenin?"

"Yeah," he says.

"Like Lenin Lenin? As in Vladimir Ilyich?"

"Yeah...like John Lennon. Anyway, he's in Make-up."

I head to Make-up. There, in the chair, is a little boy. He has a small body, like a ten-year-old's. He is sitting very still, looking straight ahead into the mirror as Make-up covers his chocolate skin with grey base. Make-up turns to me and says, "Hey, your scene was really good. I saw it the other day."

"Oh, the little speech?"

"Yeah, you looked really upset."

"Like I meant it, eh?"

"Yeah. Are you back in today?"

"No, my bit's done. I'm here to translate for Lenin."

"We'll be a little while."

In Spanish, I say, "Hi Lenin. How are you?" He says nothing but carefully moves his eyes to take in my reflection in the mirror. I tell him I'm going to be his translator. No response. I ask him if he understands. He nods his head. I tell him I'll wait for him outside.

Minutes later, a serious, entirely grey Little Lenin joins me.

"How you doing?" I ask him.

No answer.

"You want to get a drink?"

He shakes his head no.

"You want something to eat?"

"They won't need you for a while so what do you want to do? You want to go take a look on set, see what they're doing? Or you want to hang out in your trailer?"

I don't know what to make of his silence, his stillness. He's not bored; I can tell that. It's something else. Maybe he's nervous. Maybe he's getting into character. Sure. I look at him again. His eyes are dark and deep as mine shafts. His face looks old, but it could be the make-up. He could be fifteen, maybe older. It's hard to tell.

"You want a coffee?"

Shake of the head.

"A cigarette?"

He smiles and says, "No." At last, something, contact.

"Okay, so why don't we head over to the set and see what's going on?" He nods his head.

As we travel from the circus to the set, I ask him, "Where are you from?"

"Nicaragua."

Ah. I wonder if his family is Somocista, oligarchs who fled when the Sandinistas arrived. Unlikely, with a name like Lenin. Lenin is the sort of name a perfervid revolutionary would give a kid. Unless of course, it is Lennon, in which case…what? He comes from a family of Beatles fans. We wander over to the set and find Craft Services. I get a coffee and a sugar donut and persuade Lenin to have a juice. Sipping apple juice through a straw, he looks like any little kid. Any grey little kid.

We waste some time wandering around the building. Downstairs, there is a comfortable lunch room with large round tables, commodious chairs and intriguing abstract pictures on the wall. On closer examination they turn out to be forensic photographs of wounds, cuts, burns, punctures. Lenin asks what they are. I tell him they are pictures of accidents. "Doctors use them." I suggest we go back upstairs and watch them shoot a scene.

Upstairs, they're almost ready to shoot a scene in the morgue. Standing by are Alejandra (Wife) and Gloria (Rosa, the alien). Lenin and I are about to make our way over to say hello, but they are ready to shoot.

"Lock it up please." We skip over cables and equipment and find a corner where we won't be in the shot or in anybody's way but can still see the action. The scene is simple. The drawer slams shut and Rosa and Wife turn away. Rosa cries; Wife holds her up, comforts her.

I explain to Lenin, "That's your mother. You've already died and you're in that box, that drawer there. They sneak in to see your body." Lenin keeps his eyes on the camera, says nothing. I wonder if he's read the script. Doubtful. I wonder if anyone has at least explained the story to him.

"Action."

The drawer slams shut, plangent in the cold room. Rosa and Wife turn away from it, into camera. Tears course down Rosa's face. Wife's face is dry but tensed as she helps Rosa out.

"Cut. Very nice. Going again please."

Corrections are made to the lighting. The two women are told to walk more slowly.

"Action."

Again, the shutting drawer and again, Rosa cries.

"Cut!" Sound is picking up conversation from down the hall. Silence restored, they go again. The drawer slams. Rosa weeps. Wife mumbles quietly to her. Rosa bites her lip. The two women walk past the camera, out of frame. They do another take and another. Five takes so far and each one Rosa has wept her bitter tears. I feel a bit embarrassed, or surprised perhaps, by the intensity of the emotion Gloria and Alejandra generate. *Save it for the close-up, sister.*

"Very nice," says the bald director who has turned out to be a reasonable guy after all, even with his too-close-together eyes and sloppy vowels. Another take, this one the close-up. Once more, the tears. *It was something, a feeling from El Salvador.* Little Lenin watches with interest but seems unmoved, unimpressed. I ask him if he's ever been on set before. No.

His scene is next: Detective Traynor shows Chad Boswell the little boy's abandoned body in the parking lot. It takes them a while to set it up, light it, lay the dolly, get the amount of garbage just right. The director wants more garbage. Specifically he wants "noosepapers" and he wants them "flyin araown." This is one of the problems of shooting in Toronto; it's just too clean to be an American city.

"Okay, Lennon just has to lie down there, see, that pile of cardboard, it's got foam underneath so he'll be nice and comfortable. When I say action, tell him not to move. He can't move. No breathing. Okay?"

I explain it all to Lenin. He doesn't say a word. He doesn't fidget or blink when Make-up and Wardrobe come around to do finals; he takes it all with equanimity, like a professional.

"Lock it up, please."

"Rolling."

"Speed."

"And action!"

Lenin is perfectly still. He holds his breath. The camera moves up his body, then pulls back for the dialogue.

"Cut."

Minor adjustments are made. I tell Lenin to breathe. I tell him he was great. I ask if he's comfortable.

"Going again please, right away. Tell Lennon that he can't move his eyes. He's moving his eyes when they're closed, under his lids. No movement at all. Okay? He's okay?"

"Action."

They do the scene again and again. Between takes, Lenin stays on the ground: a grey little boy, lying on cardboard and garbage. During takes, he doesn't twitch, sneeze, flinch or shiver. He doesn't breathe. He doesn't move his eyes. From my vantage point, sitting on a sandbag under a lighting stand, he looks entirely convincing. There's something, the slight twist in his spine or the odd line that his arm makes, that rings true. He's a natural. This time instead of watching Lenin, I listen to the scene.

CHAD:
(*under his breath*) Jesus.

DET. TRAYNOR:
How old do you think he is?

CHAD:
Don't know. Hard to say with these people.

Good casting.

"Cut."

"Checking the gate."

The gate is clean which means Lenin is done and therefore, so am I. The First A.D. comes over to thank Lenin, shakes his hand. "Nice work, big guy." Lenin looks at his feet. On our way back to the make-up trailer, I ask him if he had fun. Lenin says, "yes," with no trace of enthusiasm.

"How long have you been here?"

"I don't know," he tells me.

"I mean in Canada."

"I don't know."

I can't tell whether he doesn't understand my Spanish or if he's being deliberately evasive. For a moment, I consider the possibility that he is too young to have a clear sense of time, but that's plainly absurd, he is at least ten years old. "Has it been a long time? Have you spent a winter here? Or did you only arrive a few months ago?"

"I don't remember," he says.

It wasn't rational. How old do you think he is? Hard to tell. The evening wind fingers the collar of my jacket. I shudder involuntarily. Before we get to Make-up I ask if his parents are coming to pick him up.

"My parents are dead."

We stand for a moment beside the Make-up trailer, the little grey boy and I, regarding each other under the purpled sky. I feel like picking Little Lenin up and hugging him but, across the street, someone lugging cable laughs and the moment passes. Instead, I open the door to the trailer. Make-up takes him, plunks him in the chair and begins to wipe off his grey skin. Axel tells me that Lennon's aunt is waiting for him when he's done.

I wait for Make-up to finish and make sure that Lenin signs his time sheet, "To make sure they pay you." Then I leave, running.

Meteorite

Darkness engulfs the headlights. He cannot make out the terrain but knows what he would see. Everywhere it is the same: emptiness of the stubbled fields, empty promises of the billboards.

He reaches into his jacket pocket, pulls out the ragged envelope. Flicks on the interior light to read the address again, slaps the envelope against the steering wheel, then folds and returns the envelope to the pocket in his jacket. He recalls the letter, the shock of it. The disorder it unleashed. He mistakenly identifies the agitation in his stomach as hunger.

"You come a fair ways," the old man with the baseball hat sitting by the window says.

"Yeah, got a way to go still."

"Yeah?"

"Yeah."

He orders coffee and pie. He eats, drinks a second cup of coffee. Thinks about smoking. Quit now three years but still, occasionally, he desires one, to fill in time. Like a companion. But no.

"That's a Valiant then," the old man says, indicating Miles' car with a nod.

"It is."

The old man speaks slowly, pausing between phrases. "Noticed you right away when you come in. Good cars. I used to drive one. Nice car. Course that was some time ago. Then I noticed your plates. Got a lot of Valiants up your way?"

"I don't know. It's used. Got it cheap. It's a good no-nonsense car."

"Run good?"

"So far."

"Yeah. You drive all the way from Canada?"

"Yeah."

He declines a third cup of coffee, then changes his mind. Regards the oily rainbow swirling against the black liquid, sinks his spoon and dispels the mirage.

"My name's Cormac," the old man says.

"That's an interesting name. Cormac?"

"Irish. Where you heading?"

Miles frowns slightly, looks into his coffee cup.

"You mind me asking?"

"No." Miles pauses, deciding. "California."

"Oh. You do have a ways to go."

Miles wants the man to ask something else. He likes this reluctant conversation. It reminds him of something. It feels good. How to prolong this? What if the old man goes?

"I have...family there," Miles says and notes that a light sweat has broken out on his brow.

"You don't look like a Canadian," Cormac says.

"Pardon me?"

"You don't look like a Canadian."

"What does a Canadian look like?"

"No offence. Just saying. You look Mexican, those dark eyes, straight black hair. Good people. Lotta folks now got a thing about Mexicans, not me. Worked alongside 'em for years. Hard workers. You ever pick fruit?"

"No."

"That's hard work. Up at dawn, work all day. The heat, the smell. Break your back, your arms. Don't get much harder." The old man adjusts his baseball cap. "You know they used to spray that uh chemicals, pesticides, down around us when we was working. Make you sicker'n a dog. Sting your eyes, your skin. Wind'd pick it up, carry it, you know, for miles. Poison. We didn't know. Nobody knew. Where they at?"

"Sorry?"

"Your family, where're they at?"

"California."

"Big place, California."

Miles tells him the name of the town. Cormac nods. Miles reaches into his jacket pocket to extract the letter and confirm the address but stops himself. Lets his fingers rest in the pocket, tracing the unstuck edges of the stamp. He wants to tell the old man that he hasn't seen his father in years. Wants to show him the letter. Wants to ask him why we are sometimes compelled to do things we do not entirely understand. Why we pursue attachments and notions that are, Miles feels, surely arrayed in failure. But he does not know how to ask these questions.

"You in some kind of trouble?" The old man is unexpectedly standing over Miles's table, a tall and crooked shadow between Miles and the light.

"No," Miles jerks his head dismissively, "I'm a cop."

"Don't mean you can't be in trouble."

"I'm not in any trouble. I'm fine."

"You know Jesus will hear your prayers. He'll help you bear that burden."

Ordinarily Miles would reject a similar suggestion but even though he does not for a moment believe that Jesus will help him, he does not become abrupt or defensive. He looks up at the man in the baseball cap and thinks about how to answer him, says, "Amen."

"You take care." Cormac nods, adjusts his baseball cap again.

"You too."

He drives on through the night, windows rolled up, the dash board a constellation, thinking on Jesus and fruit pickers; and Cormac; and Debbie, his ex-wife who was never really his wife; and how he has become his father, delinquent; how people without warning, without knowing, become what they become as if there were truly an infinite and mysterious plan or, as the Greeks believed, women who spin fates like spiders spin their silken traps.

He drives into the next day, the next state, stopping only to use washrooms, get gas and coffee. The farther south he drives the more unsettled he feels. The moment he learned that his father had died something in him began to fall, a slow controlled fall, an arc like that described by divers who leap from rock cliffs. He does not know what is falling, nor when nor where it will land. He knows only that something is falling and that the fall is now less and less controlled. The parabola disintegrates, the rate of descent increases. His upper back aches, fingers cramp, eyes burn with fatigue. He leaves the highway and drives into the city.

Abandoned buildings, the devastated blocks. The wasted centres of cities as if bomb-damaged. Everywhere the collapse of civic projects and great public dreams. Everywhere the retreat to the private spheres of family and the self. Even there, chaos and danger. The further retreat into silence and ruined sleep, nightmares.

He cruises the downtown core looking for a sign, some indication of where he should stop. Where he can eat, drink, rest. He watches the people on the sidewalks, stopping, turning, talking, laughing, hurrying, making deals and promises. Obeying the compulsion, the great current that orders them to survive, lie, win. Two white kids dash out in front of his car. He punches the brakes. They yell at him, vanish laughing.

He regards the hookers. They see him drive by slowly, try to work up some enthusiasm for him, smile. He pulls up to the curb, one approaches. He rolls down his window, almost badges her, stops himself. She leans in the window.

"Hi." Her eyes search out the car interior, professional.

"Hi," he says. Her eyes are blue, her hair dry and dyed. But she looks fine, not like some that resemble garish skeletons, too long at it or ruined by some habit. He wants to reach out, feel the warmth of blood beneath her skin.

She smiles, asks if he wants a date. He asks does she know where to eat around here.

"What are you talking about?"

"Are you hungry? Do you want to eat?"

"Baby, you wanna buy me supper? I don't think so. I'm working. I'm not allowed to eat on the job." She laughs extravagantly. He smiles. He likes the way she looks.

"What's your name?"

"April."

"April, that's pretty."

"So honey, you wanna have some fun?" She is losing interest; he sees her watching the cars that pass even as she talks to him. He feels disappointment, resentment. Foolish.

"I gotta eat."

"Okay. Well maybe you wanna come after your supper and see me." She withdraws her head from the car and waves to him as he pulls away.

Chewing an enormous steak, drinking weak American beer, he names the feeling in his abdomen. "I'm sick to death of hanging out with myself, that's all. Bored. I need some company, some distraction." He mumbles this to himself as he eats.

He traces his boredom deeper and discovers a rank pool in his gut. He calls this place loneliness, even though it is full of people. His father is there, come back from the dead to castigate him. His sisters and their husbands are there, their successful families, their houses in green suburbs. His partners from work are there with their drinks and jobs on the side, their jokes and blowjobs during coffee breaks. Debbie's nervous hands are there. And guys from high-school and girls and even Mr. Fowler, the P.E. teacher is there. He feels he has never grown up, never graduated. An impostor in a world of capable adults.

He will go back to see April. He thinks about sex with her. He imagines various positions, the noises they might make. It is interesting to think about. It distracts him. But he has had sex with hookers before and knows the most interesting part of it is before. Is the imagining of it. The choosing. The anticipation. Sex with hookers, sex itself maybe, is a promise that cannot be delivered. Because it ends. She will take her money and go. They will wipe themselves and carry on, separately, unchanged. Though there is that moment, he thinks, that swimming and singing, when everything fades, when the world dissolves. But it is only a moment. The world always returns.

Perhaps she will talk with him a few moments or longer. Perhaps he can show her the letter, confess to her the dread in his heart. But he recognizes that April will only talk to him because he pays her. She does not want to talk to him; she wants his money. That is the deal, the arrangement; the lie they agree to.

It occurs to him that money tarnishes every action; that disappointment attends every enterprise; that life is a series of promises unmet. Miles is a big man in a checked, red shirt sitting hunched in a small chair. Around him tables hum with conversation and activity which he cannot penetrate. He is a red speck that chews meat in a cosmos dim and indifferent.

He goes to a motel, masturbates, sleeps erratically, wakes early and continues.

Driving slowly now, only a mile or so from her house, their house. He imagines his body is a dark galaxy, a parallel universe. His organs are blood red stars and the car with him inside is a meteorite falling through the infinite blackness. He shakes with increasing violence until he is forced to pull the car over and retch dryly in the street. She, in turn, feels slightly dizzy when she sees him alight from the car, as if he had not died, only gone to the mall for a paper. She steadies herself against the door frame, does not know where to look when he appears before her. She says, "You must be Emilio. Gave me such a shock when I seen you get out from the car. You look…. Excuse me, I'm Linda…. Please," she manages finally, "come in."

The house is small and tired but clean. Everywhere there are photographs of his father and this woman which Miles can only glance at. His father seems small. Smaller and happier. There are knickknacks and mirrors and figurines everywhere and on the wall of the living room a framed piece of embroidery that reads: Friends are Hugs for the Heart. She seats him at the kitchen table, brings food, beer, talks continuously.

"Well, I am so glad to finally know you. You're a good-lookin' boy, just like your...Berto." She smiles warmly but her arms remain wrapped around her. "Yes, I am glad though I'm sorry it hadda be this way. Life is funny. It's hard. It doesn' always give us what we want, what we expect. But it does bring us things, chances, and we have to see those and take 'em. I think you know what I mean."

"I won't lie to you Emilio. It's not just cause you look so much like Berto that I'm feelin' nervous. Though, seein' you there so polite, sittin' at the kitchen table, I know there's nothin' really to worry 'bout. But...." She drinks. "I wasn't sure 'bout lettin' you all know when Berto died. I thought maybe better just let...." she waves her hand vaguely, "but I thought, no, they were his children.... I wrote the letter 'bout six weeks after but it was another month after that I sent it."

Miles nods, drinks, takes the letter out of his jacket, places it on the table before them. She does not seem to notice it.

"I seen you lookin' at the pictures on the wall when you come in. We were happy together. Your father was happy. We had a good life. I know that must be hard to...well, I don't know what really. But I know you must have your feelin's 'bout your father and what he did and didn't do. And that's fine. Everybody has feelin's. But you can' judge him. You don' know what was in his heart. Or mine. Only the Lord can judge. You want another beer?"

"I didn't come here to judge you," Miles says.

"I know that."

"I don't know why I came here." He looks at her and she turns away, fixing a fallen strand of her long hair. He does not know what to think of her. She is not, of course, what he expected. She is plump, unadorned, wears glasses, walks like she wears boots. Old. His father looks happy in the photographs. He remembers his father as a worried, sullen man.

"That's at the Christmas party. That year your dad was Santa Claus. Funniest thing. The Mexican Santa."

He spends the day silent and nervous in the cramped house, his guts roiling with anger, fear and confusion. She calls him Emilio, a name he has not heard or used in years. He is embarrassed by this woman's volubility and disturbed by the ubiquitous evidence of her intimacy with his father. He imagines his father entering or leaving the house, reclining in a chair, perhaps the one he is sitting in now. He is glad he cannot see the bedroom. In the bathroom, he finds his father's razor with black hairs stuck to it. He holds it a moment, considers taking it. There are more photographs. A snapshot of his father in a suit standing beside a small brown woman in a colourful dress. They pose stiffly in front of a grubby church under an unblemished, cerulean sky. Miles stands, his pants around his ankles, trying to reconstitute his father's life from these strands. He can connect nothing, understand nothing.

He asks her about the photograph of his father in the suit. "Oh, I don' know who that is. That was down...he went down to Morelos 'bout ten years ago. I didn' go. I don' remember who that is. His sister maybe?"

Later, she gets a little drunk and cries. She tells Miles that his father had a sadness she could never ease, touch. She tells him that he was kind and good; that he worked hard; that he found God; that she misses him; that they danced together; he was a good dancer. She tells him how he died.

"He knew. The doctors'd say he was gonna sorta walk but he knew. He knew. And he didn' want to live like that, crippled. So he made a decision. I know that. He wouldn't take any...nourishment? He decided. It was awful, Emilio." She wipes her eyes. "He just got skinnier 'n skinnier and his eyes got softer and softer. And one day, he was gone. He's gone. But he decided. I think the Lord can understand that. The Lord will forgive him that. I pray that the Lord will forgive him that. But I'm not afraid of dyin' anymore. I'm not. Because death is just the place of reunion and release from sufferin' and loneliness. D'you know?"

Miles does not, but hopes she's right. They eat a silent dinner. It grows darker outside and Miles insists he should be on his way. She protests. "What would your father say? Turn you out of the house this hour? You'll be comfortable here." Shows him the TV room, the couch that folds out. "Get an early start, fresh."

She returns with blankets and says, "Here," offering a man's watch. "Take it. I know he would have wanted you to have it." Miles holds the watch in his big hand, scrutinizes the unmoving hands, the roman numerals on the dial.

"Needs windin'," she says, taking it back, winding it. "There. It's a good watch. He would have wanted you to have it." Miles nods his head, puts the watch to his ear. She says, "I expect I won't be seein' you in the mornin'. You help yourself to whatever you like. There's coffee in the big tin on the counter, milk in the fridge, sugar in the bowl by the tins. Well, goodnight."

He stops her before she turns away.

"Linda, I uh didn't know really why I was coming here. I just felt I had to. I'm glad you sent the letter. I'm feeling a lot of things that I can't...mixed feelings and I...He...I have a lot of resentment and that towards...but I'm trying not to let anger get the best of me. I don't want—I want to know...things. About him. And us. Me. I can see from today that um...that he was a person and uh...." He wants to say something else, more, but his voice will not work. He wants to hug her.

She cries again, says, "He was afraid of you. He was so bust up 'bout leavin' you. He was so scared of you." She wipes her eyes, bites her lip, looks at Miles for a long time.

"Love is a terrible thing," she tells him and turns away. Miles closes the thin door behind her.

He wanted to be hard, cynical, a bored cop. But somewhere there is some tenderness, a wound, that seeps. He sits on the couch, his head in his hands, unsure what to do. He puts a hand to his solar plexus. He experiences his emotion as physical pain, a suffocating distress behind the enclosure of his ribs. The couch smells faintly of beer and cleanser. Crumbs are caught in the folds of the upholstery. An image of fearful gentleness appears: his father asleep on the couch, head in Linda's lap; she watches television, eats chips.

He waits until he is sure Linda is asleep then leaves the house, drives south.

Only a mile or two from the house he begins to cry. He pulls off the road onto the gravel shoulder. His crying is unpractised, horrible. His tears bruise skin; his sobs break bones. He weeps for all he has lost, squandered, never known. He weeps for want of gentleness of certainty of love. He weeps for his mother, his father, and again, himself. Drivers rushing past, tuned to midnight radio stations, do not hear his tectonic anguish.

With first light, the radio plays many songs he recognizes. The road feels good, the rhythm of driving settles in his body. The early morning is cool and the world seems less tired. Now he finds a station that plays boleros and corridas and takes it for a sign. He cannot understand the words of the songs though he knows most of them are songs that tell of violent ends and leaving everything you know and the others are songs of loves lost and loves betrayed. He knows this because of the way the singers' voices throb and break and, in the end, what else is there to sing about?

He takes the photograph of his father and his aunt from his shirt pocket and places it in the glove compartment together with the watch and the letter, his passport and revolver and badge. He imagines a strange alchemy as he closes the compartment. He thinks: I'll open that later and find a rabbit.

He will enter Mexico through Tijuana. He has pictures of Tijuana, ideas about it, from movies. He imagines a city distended with corruption and squalor. He knows this picture is not entirely accurate. He imagines alongside the picture of Tijuana, another picture, also inaccurate, of Morelos. It is green there and quiet. Following the trail of his unrest, guided by the photograph he has stolen, he will find the green and quiet place with the worn church and boundless sky. There, in Morelos, a place he has never seen nor heard of, he believes he will rest.

The Dream Of The Library

It was our last day there and we had decided—the emblematic nature of the decision was not entirely apparent to me at the time[1]—to spend it apart. Beatrice[2] was going, with my cousin Mario, to buy (on credit) the leather jacket we had seen while window shopping in the Recoleta district, and I was going to go to the *Biblioteca Nacional* in search of an apocryphal book by an obscure, and, perhaps justifiably, forgotten poet. This book made mention—and this was the reason for my interest in it—of my great-grandfather.

Books were not a significant part of my childhood, but there were three titles that my parents often referred to, and, consequently, had become important to me. We did

---

1. I had written in my journal:

    It's not going well. We didn't prepare or plan for this very well. It's not what I expected. We bicker about every little thing. Not understanding what's being said is very frustrating for B. It's frustrating for me, though I won't admit to her that I don't always understand what's going on. Mario though has been very helpful since we arrived. Taken Bea under his wing. Showing her around: clubs and performance art things that don't interest me. Soon be home. Soon be over.

2. Not her real name. Obviously.

not own copies of these books and this fact contributed to their significance; they were incorporeal, mysterious. Of the three, José Hernández's famous epic poem, *Martín Fierro*, was referred to the most often. My parents could, and would, recite long passages of it, with fingers and eyebrows raised to indicate emphasis, in measured, rising and falling cadences. (I can still hear them: *Aquí me pongo a cantar / a compás de la vigüela....*) Written in an octosyllabic verse filled with archaic words and non-standard inflexions, *Martín Fierro* proved difficult to read. Nevertheless, I cried at the end when Fierro and his friend, Cruz, were forced to flee, crossing the border into *terra incognita*, to escape the injustice that pursued them.

The second book was Anatole France's acerbic satire, *The Island of the Penguins*, which my father customarily mentioned whenever broad questions of a sociological, judicial, historiographical, or theological nature arose. When I finally read the book for myself, I found it had more to tell me about my father than anything else.

The third book was of maternal provenance. When I was quite young—four, or five, or six—my mother would tell me stories about her grandfather. They took place in and around Palermo, a rough neighbourhood in Buenos Aires, where, she said, he lived and worked. The stories almost always included a knife fight from which my great-grandfather invariably emerged justified, victorious, and impeccable in his Victorian apparel. They were sensational, violent stories, and naturally, I loved them. Finally settling under the sheets, I would ask if the story was true and she would assure me it was, stating, "*Hasta escribieron un libro.*" It was in a book, she claimed, "*El libro de mi abuelo.*" Thus, The book of my grandfather, (my mother's grandfather) completed the curious trinity of texts.

I outgrew bed-time stories eventually, and the book, which corroborated them, entered my thoughts only occasionally. My brothers, younger than I, never mentioned it or the stories, and I became convinced that the book, like so many images associated with my childhood, was something I had dreamed or invented. I forgot about it. However, one afternoon while preparing dinner, my father playfully waved a knife, and, with a jolt, the wonderful bed-time stories instantly and collectively returned to me. I asked my father what he knew about my great-grandfather. He promptly disabused me of the notion that my great-grandfather was a gallant gentleman who reluctantly wielded a knife when his honour or that of a gentle lady was insulted. My father used the words *compadrito* and *matón*, and I managed to piece together that my great-grandfather had been involved in racketeering and strong-arm stuff. My father couldn't tell me much else.

The book of my grandfather rose from the depths of my memory where it had lain submerged for years. The book (or its image) had become numinous: a repository of history, blood, meaning. Too isolated in my ruminations, too embarrassed perhaps, by my confused feelings surrounding the book, I did not ask my mother to confirm or deny its existence until many years later.

When I finally did ask her about it, a look came over her face that can only be accurately described as wistful. She told me that yes, the book was real; she had seen a copy of it when she was young, but had no idea what might have become of that copy. She admitted that the book was not about her grandfather, but that it contained a verse, a page, perhaps an entire chapter, dedicated to him. She told me that the book was actually called *Las Esquinas de Palermo* (The Street-Corners of Palermo) and that it had been written by a poet whose name she believed was Macedonio Almafuerte. She acceded that her grandfather had been, for at least part of his life, a disreputable character.

Any mention of my great-grandfather, tango, knife fights, or any other folkloric charms, which I (stupidly) half-expected to find in the cosmopolitan city of Buenos Aires, met with Mario's silence and Beatrice's disdain. I agreed with her, to a great extent, that these were tired, macho tropes, but could not deny the powerful hold they exerted on my imagination. In Buenos Aires, our vacation rapidly decomposing in the humidity, I became convinced that finding the book could redeem my, our, trip.

The library, located on calle Mexico, was, a stately, turn of the century structure. Inside, I was quickly overwhelmed by the vertiginous quantity of books housed there. I had no idea where to look, nor how to proceed. I knew I probably would not be permitted to simply pull the book from a shelf. Most likely I would have to ask for it and a librarian or clerk would be sent to fetch it from a remote and musty corner of the building. I felt embarrassed by the thought of asking for the book. I wasn't sure of the author's name. They would, undoubtedly, ask why I wanted the book, or with what institute I was associated. I felt certain I would be ignored, or humiliated, in some small but significant way. I decided to walk about and reconnoitre in the hope that I might learn something about the arrangement and operation of the library that might mitigate or forestall any embarrassment.

I climbed a spiral staircase and soon became lost within the maze of narrow and poorly lit corridors. It was pleasant enough, innocently wandering the rows and rows of books, but a familiar feeling of impatience and frustration came over me, and I began to worry that I might never find the book and, therefore, not redeem my trip. I decided to find my way back to the central information desk, and request assistance. If they asked, I would lie and tell them I was a student at a Canadian university doing some preliminary research for a paper. I made my way down the spiral staircase and found myself in yet another lightless corridor. I cursed, out loud, confusedly, and in English, "Jesus Christ, who designed this place, Kafka's architect?"

A voice in the darkness said, "Pardon me?"

I apologized and explained that I had become disoriented. A figure emerged out of the murky shadows. I could make out a rather large head above a round body in a dark and formless suit. He was an old man, maybe in his seventies. "What are you looking for?" he asked. I told him I wanted the main desk and he said he would take me there. I thanked him, and made a comment about the labyrinthine configuration of the library. He laughed briefly, and said that it would take a lifetime to learn its multitudinous circuits.

He trundled down a book-lined corridor, at the end of which was a small reading desk tucked into an illuminated corner, and, apologetically, asked if I'd mind very much if he sat for a moment or two to rest before undertaking the perilous journey to the information desk. I said I did not mind at all. I got a good look at him there and realized, with unpleasant surprise, that he was blind, or nearly so. His eyes, the right one half-concealed under a lethargic eyelid, were dull and focused on nothing. I said, "You speak English very well."

"So do you," he replied. I smiled and struggled to find an appropriate and witty reply but nothing occurred to me. "My forefathers were English," he said. "It is a marvellous tongue. Keats, Shelley, Swineburne, Shakespeare, Johnson, Kipling, Wells, Poe, Stevenson, Chesterton, James, Twain...." He named a long list, nodding slightly and smiling fondly at each name.

He apologized again for having to rest and told me of a broken stairway elsewhere in the library that had "almost killed" him. I nodded, then, realizing my gesture was meaningless to him, uttered something solicitous. He asked me what had brought me to the library.[3]

"Oh," I hesitated but decided there was no reason not to tell this man the truth, "I'm looking for a book. A particular book that...my mother...a book that mentions my great-

---

3. I do not claim to have remembered our conversation word for word, but I assure the reader that I am true to the tone and content of our dialogue.

grandfather. It's personal. A family thing." He nodded his head and said nothing, as if expecting me to go on. "My mother used to tell me stories about my great-grandfather. He was some kind of small-time criminal apparently. *Un compadrito*." He smiled at the phrase then turned his face with its thick features toward me. "I thought it might be...I don't know...I thought I should try to find the book. It feels important to me. To find it, I mean."

He indicated that he agreed, "Of course."

I felt something akin to guilt, that I could take him in, study, scrutinize him: his thick eyebrows, his over-large nose, his white hair pulled back behind his ears, his thick hands resting on his cane, while to him I could not be much more than an indistinct shadow. I looked away. He asked if I was a tourist; I told him I was. I found myself telling him about the trip and how it had not worked out quite the way I had hoped it might. I confessed my disappointment at being unable to uncover any of the rustic and exotic delights the city might hold. "I wasn't really prepared. I read all the wrong books. *Martín Fierro* doesn't prepare you for contemporary Buenos Aires." This thought amused him. "Neither do my parents' accounts. I think I've been looking for a city that no longer exists, or ceased to exist some time ago. I have the wrong map, you know?"

He said, "I love maps," and I wondered what he meant but was too shy or embarrassed to ask him about it. "What is the name of the book?" he asked. I told him. I added that I thought the author's name was Macedonio Almafuerte. "Yes," he said, "that's right." I disbelieved what I'd heard. I asked him if he knew the book and he said he did. "It's not very good but there was a time when I read that sort of thing." And then he recited several verses of something—I don't know what it was—a *milonga*[4] perhaps, written in an argot that I did not

---

4. A song form which preceded the tango.

understand, about a man who knew that death was waiting for him, and went to meet it with his knife in hand.

He sat quietly for a moment after the recitation, and I didn't know what to say. He said, "Yes, it is an unhappy city now; these are dark days."[5] And then, without pausing, he began speaking of Palermo, the neighbourhood my great-grandfather lived in, and its environs. He told me that it was eponymously named after a sixteenth-century landowner, and not, as I believed, the Sicilian city. There was a river, he said, now underground. There was a garrison. He told me of the brothels and bars, and the tangos that were born in them: that sentimental, nostalgic discourse of the city and its loneliest children; a music as profligate and sorrowful as the men and women who danced and composed it. He told me of the heroic knife fights in the tenebrous docks, the glinting blades describing mortiferous arcs. He depicted a complete and extinct universe: long skirts, elaborate hats, hair brilliantined with macassar oil, polished black buttoned boots and moustaches, double breasted jackets, black hats always cocked to one side; cafés and games of *truco*; cramped houses; horses drawing streetcars (number 64, he said), open carriages, and wagons bearing poetic inscriptions: "See You in the Morning," "Where are you now?" or, "The New Moon;" exuberant Italians in the jumbled and dusty streets.

"It's changed now," he said. "Even when I lived there, some years after your maternal great-grandfather, it wasn't quite as colourful. Though the zoo was marvellous. It smelled of tigers and candies."

He sat thinking silently, then murmured, "A city that no longer exists in a book that has almost been forgotten. Delightful." Then he continued in a slightly stronger voice,

---

5. A reference to his sightlessness, or something else?

"Sometimes, I have the sensation that there is not a single city left, that all cities have vanished. In the end, all cities are fictions sustained by dreamers." He re-gripped the handle of his cane and shifted in his seat. "I've detained you long enough. I can take you directly to the book you're looking for if you like. Follow me." I wanted to talk further, to ask questions, but he stood and began to make his way through the narrow corridors with disconcerting speed. He opened doors without hesitation, and passed quickly through dim rooms where more books were stored. I found it difficult to keep up. "Not long now," he would call over his shoulder, or, "almost there." To orient himself, he would, at irregular intervals, reach up and pull a book off the shelf, bring it to his nose to read the title, then replace it, and set off again.

After climbing several flights of stairs and traversing what felt like leagues of confined corridors, he finally stopped and turned to me, "You should find it at the end of this aisle, on the second shelf from the bottom, somewhere in the last half of the shelf." He said he wasn't going to accompany me because such encounters could only be made alone. I thanked him. I wanted to hear more from him but didn't know how to say so, and wasn't even sure what it was I wanted him to tell me. The moment passed. He extended a large, soft hand, and I took it and shook it. Then, he turned and faded into the shadows of the library. I was left, alone, regarding the rows of books. A succession of contradictory and powerful emotions gripped me: I felt strangely deflated then, delighted, then apprehensive. When I came to the end of the aisle, I felt almost weary.

Earlier, I had considered stealing the book if I ever came across it. Now I knew I couldn't do that. I found *Las Esquinas de Palermo* more or less where he said it would be. It was worn and broken, but the title was legible on its cover. I touched the letters gently but my psychometric abilities, such as they may be, perceived no pulse; there was no disturbance in the ether. I realized that I no longer had any need of *Las Esquinas de Palermo*. I knew enough. The old man had, as far as was possible, redeemed my trip. I returned the book to its place on the shelf without having opened it, and easily made my way out of the library.

I walked for a long time in the soft afternoon air, in no particular direction, with no particular plan. The light grew thicker and more golden. Everything shimmered softly in the warm and dusty sunlight, as if magically rendered insubstantial. I found a café and went in. From my seat by the window, I watched the swallows swooping into and out of the dirty cornices, and was overcome by an inexplicable sense of loss for the passing of something, an epoch or world I had not known. I thought of Carthage, of Babylon, of Tenochtitlán. I thought of my great-grandfather and Galicia; I thought of all the places I would not see and all the things I would not do in my brief lifetime. I thought of the clarity and blueness of Beatrice's eyes. I became acutely aware of my mortality there in the window of that insignificant cafe. Eventually, I broke free of my reverie, and returned to the world of clocks, newspapers, automobiles, and marriages.

That night, we had dinner with my Tia Sara. Cousin Mario managed to join us for this, our farewell dinner. Tia Sara asked about our last day and I explained that we'd spent it apart. Beatrice showed us her new leather jacket, which met with approval from all, especially Mario who applauded and whistled and kissed her affectionately when she returned to the table. Tia Sara asked me what I had bought. I told them that I had spent most of the day wandering the National Library. She knew something about my interest in the obscure book and asked if I had found it. I explained that at the last minute I had decided not to look at it. I explained, in English and Spanish that I couldn't risk the disappointment. I felt that the book could never equal what I imagined. I preferred my notional text. I told them too about the old man I had met, and how he told me, revealed to me, what I knew the book could not; how he had shown me around the library, directed me, in fact, to the very book I sought. Tia Sara looked at me sceptically. She asked me to describe him and the details of our conversation again. I did so. She asked Mario if he thought I was acting. Mario asked Beatrice and she said she didn't think so.

Then Tia Sara said, "*Me vas a decir que lo viste a Borges en la Biblioteca?*"

I said I didn't know. I told her I didn't recognize the name she had given. She excused herself from the table. I translated my aunt's rhetorical question to Beatrice and told her the name she had used, Borges, didn't mean anything to me. Tia Sara returned with a book, opened to a black and white photograph. It was him, the man in the library, a younger version of him, but, unmistakably, the blind man who had led me through the corridors.

"Borges," she said. Argentina's greatest writer. She enumerated his books.

I said, "Wow. Cool."

Tia Sara looked at me as if I were an idiot. "*Murió hace años.*" I didn't believe her and asked her to repeat what she'd said. She repeated it word for word, but louder. Since I had no reply, Tia Sara turned to Mario and indicated he should translate for Beatrice. He gently stroked her hand to get her attention and said, "Borges, he is famous writer of Argentina. But he is dead already many years."[6]

---

6. I have since learned that Borges was director of the National Library for almost twenty years, and that two of his predecessors there were also blind.

Winter Comes To
The Edge Of The World

The smell of frying food invades her sleep. Her guts are a sea of roiling, sour waters. Everything swims. Her heavy eyelids open slowly. They close. She wants to get up. Wants to open a window but feels too weak to stand. The world is liquid, swirling and rolling. Nothing stands still. What the hell are they frying at this hour of the day? She waits, and, finally, the revulsion passes. She gets out of bed, raises the window, breathes deeply.

Armando.

Tomás.

Fernando.

Rodolfo.

Julio is not on the couch. Of course. Because Julio left. Weeks ago. Julio went back. In the kitchen, she drinks water, slowly eats a piece of bread. She checks the time on the stove clock.

She remembers. She has asked Alicia to take her to the Tower. *La Torre CN. El Lapis. El Pico.* She wants to have a better picture of the city. She washes and dresses quickly but not carelessly. She takes the subway. It is clean, the subway. They're very proud of that here. Nobody looks at you. They're probably proud of that too.

Alicia, impeccably groomed as always, pays. They go up. Cecilia looks out. She sees the repeated grids, the pattern. As she thought. She asks Alicia if Winnipeg looks like this too. "*No sé.* I don't know." Alicia, who is familiar with Cecilia's odd questions, her non-sequiturs, still cannot resist asking Cecilia why she thought Winnipeg might look like Toronto. Cecilia says, "Curiosity."

When she was in the *pozo* the man from the Canadian Embassy had said, "Winnipeg. We think we can get you to Winnipeg. Would you like to go there?" Cecilia said yes, not knowing what Winnipeg meant. Once, when things seemed to be moving toward her release, the man asked her if she had ever committed any crimes. He explained they couldn't take her if she had committed crimes. She looked at him, uncomprehending. He asked too if she had been maltreated, if she needed anything. She never knew how to answer those questions so she pretended not to understand him. The man was either very subtle or very stupid.

Marta.

Graciela.

Liliana.

She looks into Alicia's intensely green eyes and smiles, then kisses her on the cheek. "*Gracias.*" The mingled scents of Alicia's deodorant and perfume momentarily upset Cecilia's stomach. Alicia smiles back at her, picks a piece of lint from Cecilia's sweater, and asks if they can go down now.

They sit at a table with large styrofoam cups of coffee between them.

"*Viste el* lawyer?"

"No, I do not see *el* lawyer."

"Have not. I have not seen *el* lawyer."

"Yes. I have not see *el* lawyer."

They enjoy the English game, and sometimes Cecilia deliberately makes mistakes to amuse Alicia. Alicia worries about Cecilia. Now that Julio is gone, Cecilia is alone too often. Alicia cannot see Cecilia as much as she'd like and worries that Cecilia has no one to talk to—she certainly won't talk to the social services people. She hasn't even told Alicia yet. Alicia knows, or guesses, some of it, but doesn't insist. She knows, however, that Cecilia must begin to talk about it. She must put words to it, name it, so that she can transfer it outside her body. Or it will become, as in Nelson's case, a kind of cancer: a despair that metastasizes.

She reaches out and gives Cecilia's skinny arm a squeeze, asks if Cecilia misses Julio. Cecilia shrugs, gives her head half a shake while running a hand through her hair. She never felt strong affection for Julio; she doesn't miss him the way people normally miss their friends, in the way she is sure she once missed people. She and Julio were thrown together by circumstance. They grew accustomed to one another and comforted one another in awkward, wordless ways. Julio's presence, the sounds he made in the apartment, seemed to keep the more desperate sensations at bay. Cecilia and Julio had been a provisional couple, a temporary alliance against the injuries and anguish of exile.

"How is your sister?" Cecilia asks.

"Nora?"

"*Cómo está?* Do you have some news?"

Alicia tells her that Nora is fine, happy in Spain. The baby is wonderful. Not a baby anymore, two years old already. And Pablo has finally found a good job and is learning to speak with a lisp to fit in with the Spaniards. They laugh. Cecilia surprises Alicia by asking her if she has any pictures of her sister and the baby. Alicia pulls some from her smart handbag.

Cecilia walks part of the way home, up Yonge, then along Bloor. She stops in a drug store. The quantity of things: devices, powders, ointments, creams, remedies.... There are pills for everything. She buys a home pregnancy test kit, and takes the clean subway home.

Two blue stripes. Positive. Unless she's misunderstood the directions. She checks the box again, and with the aid of her dictionary, re-reads the instructions. The second blue stripe means positive. She doesn't know what she thinks or feels. Not yet. She studies the tester, regards it closely as if it might reveal more. Perhaps it is wrong.

Julio, she'll have to tell Julio. Somehow. When he gets in touch. If he gets in touch. She cannot think. Too many questions. Too many problems. Contradictions. She won't think about it right now. She is very tired. There is the bulletin to distribute, there is work to do, but Cecilia lies down on the broken couch and closes her eyes, squeezing the plastic test kit in her left hand. It must be a mistake. She will do the test again. It can't be true. Who will help her? She would cry if she were not so choked with confusion.

Cecilia could tell Alicia but Alicia would demand explanations, justifications. Alicia would find fault, lay blame. Cecilia cautions herself to think carefully, proceed slowly. There is nothing to tell. Yet. It is only a test. Two blue stripes, a chemical reaction, nothing more.

She will have to end it. Alicia is right. It is too complicated, too difficult, unfortunate, the worst possible timing. She can barely look after herself. And this is no world for children.

It is a fine evening, warm and dry. She takes a stack of bulletins and goes to distribute them in front of the library. Suddenly, the world is full of children. Everywhere today she has seen pregnant women; young mothers pushing pudgy babies in strollers, or carrying them in packs; fathers cycling with children helmeted and strapped into bicycle seats; grandparents swinging toddlers. To keep her mind occupied, Cecilia names things: street, leaves, branch, student, sidewalk, doors, backpack, purse, gloves, mouth, hat, earrings, laughter, dog shit, garbage can, red light.

Teresa.

Mario.

El Griego.

In the dream, she is in a wet cell. Though no daylight penetrates the thick and mouldering walls, she knows somehow that it is morning. She is surprised to discover that she is alone in the cell. She does not know where the others are or what has happened to them. Then a voice says, "She's awake," and she understands that she had fainted and they were only waiting for her to revive before continuing. She wakes as the electric prod approaches her damp skin.

The lights are on—she always sleeps with the lights on now. "Julio," she calls, her voice clogged with fear. There is no answer. Julio cannot hear her. He is not there on the couch. Julio has gone.

She repeats: Canada. You're safe. They can't touch you here. Canada. You're safe. They can't touch you here. She reminds herself: there are no Falcons cruising the street here; no camps.

Alfonso.

Pedro.

Martín.

Raul.

She lets the anger rise. The anger helps. Better anger than fear. She imagines revenge. She fantasizes murder, carnage, redemption. She crawls from the bed. The night is ruined, sleep lost.

She throws open the refrigerator and takes the package of cigarettes from the butter compartment. She takes a cigarette out, tosses the package onto the counter, slams the fridge door shut. With faintly trembling fingers, she lights the cigarette on the gas stove. She inhales sharply and experiences almost immediate relief.

She fills the kettle and puts it on the ring of blue flame. The hiss of the gas, the noise of a passing bus are comforting. The slight breeze stirring the humid air is soothing. The cigarette smoke curling as it rises is soothing. Her anger calms her. The bastards, motherfuckers, shit-eaters. She washes her face in the kitchen sink, dries her hands on her t-shirt. She scratches her scalp almost violently, shakes out her long brown hair. The dream falls away, dispelled by the rattling water in the kettle, the creaking of the flimsy kitchen chair, the clink of the teaspoon.

She sits down at the rickety table from *el* Honest Ed's to drink *maté* and wait for morning. In between sips, she chews her fingernails. She makes a neat pile of them. How big is it? Five weeks? Four weeks? She has never been regular, especially after. She pushes the pile of bitten off fingernails around. She smokes, twisting her face as she inhales. She taps the ash onto the table. She shivers from the cold.

When they arrived it was Christmas Eve. The wind hurled snow like insults. The world was white with snow. Then, grey when the sun fell. The streets emptied. The edge of the world, Julio said. Or maybe it was Limbo. They laughed at the absurdity, the impossibility, of it; here they were, still alive. But where was here? What was this empty, white and grey place? They laughed till tears ran down their faces and stung their skin. Exiled to the edge of the world.

Julio. Now he has gone and she has had no word from him. Except for the test. Two blue stripes. A message. Of a kind. It's funny. She laughs. Nothing surprises her. Nothing makes any sense. Anything is possible. Perhaps it was meant to be. It is so unexpected, so surprising a development that it can only be a sign: the hand of fate. But she doesn't believe in fate. Or, she didn't before. She smokes. Drinks *maté*. Minutes pass.

It is ridiculous. A mother? A single mother? In exile? No. Adoption? No. She cannot carry it in her broken body for nine months and then push it out, bloody, wet, shouting, into a stranger's hands. No.

There is no choice. She will terminate it. How do they do that here? Maybe they have a pill for it. Now she is angry again. At Julio, the shit-head, who refused to wear a condom. At herself, the shit-brain, who let him get away with it. She finishes the cigarette, leaves the filter standing on the table between the pile of ashes and the pile of fingernails. A vein in her temple begins to throb.

She cannot carry it to term. No. That is ridiculous. But neither can she abort it. The thought of a hospital suffuses her with dread. The lights, the gurney, the needles, the latex gloves, the tubes and bags of blood, the straps and clamps, the men in gowns touching her, drugging her, cutting her. The image of a doctor makes her flinch, revives sleeping wounds. The sweaty, bald bastard who came around every few hours to make sure they didn't push her too far, that they didn't lose her. She cannot go to a hospital. She cannot have a baby. She is trapped.

Cecilia feels the air in the room shudder, announcing the dread arrival of that which is worse than fear, worse than pain, worse than any dream.

The nightmares are exhausting and terrible, but they are, after all, only dreams, and she has learned to wake from them. The worst is the emptiness. She calls it *la nada*, the nothing, and can feel it stalking her, circling like a malevolent bird. Its presence is announced by headaches and the ghostly spasms of her muscles, trapped in the memory of the moment they were beaten, pricked, burned. *La nada* descends slowly, beating its ghastly, rancid, black wings. *La nada* settles, clutching her thin shoulders. Then, it enters through her ear, transforming into a grey wind that sucks and howls in the curves of her skull and ribs. *La nada* tells her lies which she is powerless to deny or refute.

La nada tells her to expect the worst; that she deserved what she got; that she was a coward to leave; that people are worse than beasts; that there is no justice and never will be; that she is less than garbage, worthless; that life is not worth living. Sometimes, *la nada* inflicts on her a parade of brutal images: truncheons; the boots of soldiers; her mother, dead; a puddle of urine; policemen behind the door; dried blood on a wooden floor; Violeta's broken face. The images, ceaselessly modulating one into another, appear inside her head. If she closes her eyes they appear more sharply. She has lost entire days in this way, unable to work or eat.

The smell of cooking oil from downstairs incites her nausea. Her body demands attention, revolts against the paralyzing horror. She feels her guts might give way. Cecilia vomits in the sink. Morning sickness releases her from *la nada*.

Days pass and she tells no one. Not Alicia, not her worker, not her sister in the note she sends. There is nothing to tell yet. She still has time. At least a month, six weeks. She is often nauseous in the mornings but learns that eating small quantities of crackers at regular intervals diminishes the feeling. She sleeps late and takes naps. Days go by and she does not distribute the bulletins. She does not rebuke herself for her laziness. She has always thought of her body as hard, disciplined, lean: a tool or weapon. Even after they beat it and broke it, she still thought of it as an instrument, a case for what remained of her will and intelligence. Now, she imagines her body differently; it is warm and watery, soft, surprising.

One night, she sets herself up at Yonge and Dundas and distributes all the bulletins that remain. She walks home after, even though it is raining. The rain soaks through her sweater to her skin. It is sharp, cold, exciting.

She goes to a movie with Alicia and her husband, John. She can't follow all the dialogue, but the movie is amusing and she laughs often, enjoying Alicia and John's enjoyment as much as anything the actors do on the screen. After, they go for coffee and cake, and talk. John tells Cecilia that she looks good and this comment makes Cecilia laugh for a long time.

She has not given any thought to the problem. She has begun, without realizing, to entertain the possibility of bringing it to term. The baby—sometimes she uses the word—feels like a possibility.

Against the generals and the dictatorship and their camps and torturers and detentions and disappearances, this pregnancy. Against their crusade of despair, this hope. Against their campaign of death, this life. She is surprised that she is thinking this way. She laughs, wondering if she might be devolving into a sloppy-thinking, peace-and-love, North American feminist, indulging in essentialist definitions of the feminine: nurturing, intuitive, peaceful, a-historical and ultimately, reactionary.

Yet, it seems to makes sense. Not the maternal archetype, but the baby. And beyond sense, it feels good. For the first time in years, she experiences her body as the site of some pleasure. The weight of her breasts, their tenderness, feels good. She cups them when she is alone, enjoying their substance, wondering at the transformation.

Her life has been split in two. Before, there was her will, her focus, and capacity for action. After, there was fragility, doubt, despair, the knowledge that she could be violated in unimaginable ways—not simply physically—that qualities (intangibles like will or acuity) could be broken fundamentally, beyond all hope of recovery and healing.

But. This baby begins to feel like a way to return to the earlier integrity. Against *la nada*, this baby. It is a project, a challenge, a praxis. The baby is proof that they have no hold over her; that she has power to make and shape.

A week passes. When Tito, Flaca, Margarita and Cecilia meet to prepare the next bulletin, Margarita complains about the difficulties of translation and the meagre sums the bulletin yields but Cecilia only feels optimism. Everything is useful. Everything is part of the struggle. She and Tito will go to a civic political rally next week. There, they will sell buttons with revolutionary images to raise money for Tupamaro friends in Uruguay and compañeros back home. Everything helps. She is excited, almost happy. She thinks about telling Flaca. Flaca is crazy for kids; she would think it is a fine idea. But there is nothing to tell yet. She still has time.

She could have this baby here. She has enough help. She will get a job, eventually. Once her situation is normalized. She could go back, too. Eventually. Her family would help. She doesn't have to tell Julio. Or she could tell him. He would be a good father, funny and gentle Julio. There are many possibilities. Anything is possible. Today, the first snow dusts the streets, houses and trees. The world is almost unsullied.

Cecilia takes scissors to her bangs. She considers cutting it all off, but decides instead to simply trim it all around. She buys a coat, bulky, warm. She buys woollen mittens and a hat. This new look—part-clown, part-yeti—delights her.

Mauricio.

Emma.

Simon.

Cristina.

She dreams that she is having her period.

She does not stop bleeding. She is awake and her gut is cramped with pain and the blood on the bed is hers and she is losing the baby and she is in Canada and they can still get her, like this, their reach is long and what they did to her is still happening and it is all she can do to phone Alicia and cry and cry.

When Alicia arrives she is alarmed by the blood, the stained sheets and nightie, the blots on the polyester carpeting. Alicia does not know what to do, but when Cecilia holds out her bony arms Alicia goes to her, holds her fast and close. Cecilia tells her, between sobs and howls, how they ruined her womb, how they tore her very cells with electricity, how they beat and humiliated her. She tells Alicia that she has lost her baby. She pulls the bloody sheets. Cecilia wanted to call her Violeta, after her friend, who died in the *pozo*. She cries and pulls her hair with blood-stained hands and falls against Alicia.

Alicia washes Cecilia gently, in lukewarm water, and talks to her in a hushed voice. She finds clean clothes, wraps Cecilia in blankets and puts her to bed on the couch. She lies beside her and holds her, whispers to her and strokes her hair, kisses her forehead, makes her tea, brings her cigarettes, and listens as Cecilia calls out the names of everyone she knew in detention. Alicia assures Cecilia there is no need of doctors or hospitals, tells her to rest, sleep. Alicia sets herself to watch over Cecilia through what remains of the night.

When Cecilia falls asleep, exhausted, Alicia phones John. His voice is woolly with sleep and worry. She says that things are all right. She will tell him more later. She thinks of their daughters and the thin web of tenderness that connects the four of them and radiates outward from there. That fragile compassion is not much to set against barbarity, but it may be enough. She cleans Cecilia's room, gathering the smeared sheets. As she cleans, she cries, not out of pity, but out of something akin to admiration for her friend's tremendous courage. She cannot imagine what resources Cecilia must have drawn on to care for herself, to meet for coffees, to chat and laugh, these past months. Human beings, she thinks, are miraculous. To the abominations that harmed her friend she gives not a moment's thought.

In the living room, Cecilia turns her head to the window and sees a tentative dawn begin to spread itself across the sky. The early light is milky grey. Winter has come to cover the city in forgetful snow. Winter, with its silences and small deaths, has come to soothe her. She closes her eyes. She falls back into sleep, aware of Alicia's gentle footsteps down the hall.

Peace In Ixturria

When the war ended, I returned to Ixturria. My first thought—an idle one—as I glimpsed the emerald splendours of Ixturria's coastline through the clouds, was that Torquemada might be there to meet me. He wasn't, of course. No one knew of my arrival, and I would have to make my way back into the capital unaided. I retrieved my bags without difficulty but hesitated before committing myself to the city. The air in the airport was thick and pungent, laced with sweat and diesel fumes, and I felt unsettled. I thought I'd linger to acclimatize myself somewhat before plunging into whatever lay ahead. I bought a package of cigarettes (a brand I did not recognize), asked for a coffee and sat on a rickety cane chair in the airport bar.

I lit a cigarette—a putrid, sputtering affair that refused to remain lit, ill-auguring, I thought, the changes that might lie in store—and sipped my black coffee. The coffee was as rich as my memory of it: ambrosia compared to the ersatz stuff I'd been reduced to consuming during my (self-imposed) North American exile. I wondered what awaited me beyond the relative safety of the airport; news of Ixturria had been sporadic and unreliable during the war. I could not help wondering, too, who of our circle—apart from Torquemada who had not left the country—would already be back.

I told myself it didn't matter which of them was here. I had made a quasi–promise to begin anew. The war had presented me with the perfect excuse to break from that particular set and I did not want to fall in with them again. They were, with the exception of Torquemada—who, paradoxically, had introduced me to them—an indolent lot with too much money and time on their hands. I had given free rein to my laziness long enough. My North American tarriance had given me an opportunity to observe, from a safe distance, the industry of the more or less average citizen, and I felt optimistic that I might, in imitation of what I had there witnessed, undertake my real work.

It would be difficult, of course, to resume my life in Ixturria and avoid them entirely. I resolved to be firm and set limits. I would learn to say no. If necessary, I could move to a more remote part of the country. I was unable to finish the cigarette and I left it to smoulder in the ashtray, the nearly full package beside it. I could pick up some decent cigarettes in the city. I had postponed the inevitable long enough. I had not come all the way back to Ixturria to linger indefinitely at the airport. I pushed my empty coffee cup aside, gathered my bags and set off.

Approaching the doors of the terminal building, I was accosted by the host of grey marketeers who gathered at transport termini to provide assistance and service to travellers. A car owner and I quickly settled on a price, and I was following him to his vehicle when a familiar voice called my name. I turned to see who it was and thought, "Oh no, Stetson." I smiled and waved. He made his breathless, sweaty way over.

"Hidalgo, what a surprise." We shook hands vigorously.

"Indeed it is." Our little circle had always made it a point to speak English and we fell back into old habits immediately.

"Remarkable coincidence. Have you just come in?"

"Yes," I told him, "only moments ago."

"Marvellous. You look good, old man. What a marvellous surprise. You've barely disembarked and already you are safely among friends. An auspicious beginning, don't you think?" I thought quite the opposite but I did not say so.

"It is quite a coincidence," I conceded, "landing at the same time."

"Oh, I arrived four days ago actually, but they lost my bags. I've been chasing them down all over the bloody place. They just turned up now. I came down myself to put the fear of God in them." His assistant, Carlos, was pushing several crammed-to-bursting bags on a squeaking trolley.

"They lost your bags. Well," I managed a chuckle, "It's good to know some things never change."

"I was rather hoping that sort of thing might have changed."

"I'm sure. Nothing like a good war to get the trains running on time, eh Stetson?"

My driver looked back at me with a mixture of inquisitiveness and impatience. "Did you hire a car?" Stetson asked

"Yes, I—"

"Let us drive you back."

"That's very kind but I've already agreed—"

"Never mind that." He turned to Carlos, "Take these bags, Señor Hidalgo's as well, to the car, and on the way, give Señor Hidalgo's taxi driver a few coins for his trouble. There." He indicated my driver.

Stetson blathered while we waited for Carlos to bring the car around. I let him prattle on and made the appropriate—or what I hoped were appropriate—noises from time to time. Carlos pulled up to the curb, we climbed in, and drove away from the battered airport toward the city. The area around the airport, once fertile and verdant, was despoiled; defoliated and gouged as if by malevolent, shovel-wielding titans.

"A blasted heath," I muttered, interrupting Stetson's monologue.

"Quite." The road was pocked with great craters around which Carlos effortlessly swerved. "Much of the countryside, apparently, was affected. The cacao plantations, the cane, and I suppose much of the rubber has been ruined, but the city, our end of things at least, seems to have escaped unscathed. Though I did go past your place the other day and it looks like you'll need to replace some windows. Did you let your man go when you left?" I made an indeterminate humming noise in response.

The landscape we travelled through was unreal, dreamlike. Amid the blackened rubble of destroyed buildings, a solitary wall stood, perfect and untouched, its painted exterior promoting the refreshing virtues of a particular soda. There, children played among the ruins while a pack of tatterdemalions worked under the vicious sun, salvaging what they could from the wrecks of deformed, armoured vehicles. Stetson asked, "Where have you been all this while, Hidalgo?"

"The United States of America."

"Ah, yes. And what did you there?"

"I made love to myriad doe–eyed, robust and young students of literature."

"Why did you ever come back?"

"Why did you?"

He nodded and sighed, then turned to study the landscape again. The poorer quarters that encircled the capital had been flattened. The inexpensive dwellings that once stood there—erected in a passing fit of governmental expenditure—had been replaced by even cheaper and if possible, uglier, tin shacks. Everywhere, incomprehensible graffiti flashed its illiterate messages at us.

"What do you know about the situation then, Hidalgo?"

"The situation?"

"Yes. Do you know anything...?" He indicated the vista through his window.

"I've only just arrived."

"I thought perhaps you'd have heard something...in America. I haven't had an opportunity to make many inquiries but I think that it would be to our advantage to determine, sooner rather than later, who's in charge." He reached into his breast pocket and extracted a packet of fine cigarettes. He offered me one, which I, recalling my decision to extricate myself from the social circles I had formerly moved in, declined.

"Why did you come back Hidalgo? I had the distinct impression we'd seen the last of you."

"Perhaps you have."

"What's that? One of your mystical enigmas?" I smiled. Leaning back into the upholstery, smoking languidly, Stetson indicated, with a tilt of his head, the monument at the end of the broad avenue, and said, "Look, the Great Navigator welcomes you home."

"He's still standing."

"Yes, yes, as I said, most of the city is untouched. The monuments are all intact, the jacarandas in the Plaza Independencia, see, you can just make them out," he pointed with his fleshy index finger, as if I did not know where to look. "And it appears that all the essential services are operating. Electricity, gas, and so on. We'll have to see if the other necessities are still in plentiful supply, what?" He smiled his thin-lipped smile and wiped his perspiring forehead with two fat fingers. "I'm sure Carlos will do his utmost to provide us all with the little things that make life in this remote corner of the world more bearable." He reached over with effort and tickled the back of Carlos's strong neck. Carlos did not react, only shifted his eyes to the rear-view to take us in. "No, Carlos?"

"*A sus ordenes, señor.*"

"Indeed, Carlos." He turned to me. "Lucia Estrada is here. I spoke with her briefly the other day. I don't know about the others but I will make inquiries and if we have a quorum I will convoke a meeting of our coterie. Catch up on everyone and everything."

"Excellent," I said, trying to sound as pleased by the prospect as possible.

I found it difficult to do much in the days that followed. The heat was oppressive and the mingled perfumes of the bougainvillaea and heliotrope in the garden had a soporific effect on me. I dreamily wandered the rooms of my mother's house—I still thought of it as her house—re-acquainting myself with the furniture, the paintings, the daguerreotypes of my mother's family, the carpets, the fixtures, all of it brought from Europe so many years ago.

In the study, I lingered over my cherished books. I ran my fingers along the spines and over the covers of my favourite volumes of poetry, the rare monographs on gnosticism, and tractates on the Kabbalah. I was pleased to find in the drawer of my desk—precisely where they ought to have been—notes for my book which I had stupidly neglected to pack when I fled the country two years ago. I re-read my notes carefully, and made one or two small comments in the margins.

I spent two days with my Petit Bijou. I felt, upon seeing it, immediately eager to play it but it had, naturally, gone out of tune. I found a tuner who promised to come later in the day and spent the hours preceding his arrival anxiously cleaning the piano and what had been the nursery, where it lived, in anticipation of playing it. Most of the following day passed in a dreamy state of nostalgia as I played all the pieces I could recall having played on it as a child. It was a delightful toy, the only child's piano in Ixturria, and had a light touch and surprisingly good tone.

I hired my gatekeeper back and he—capable fellow—brought his son—another capable fellow—around to help clean the place up. A glazier came to repair the windows. Friday morning, one of Stetson's houseboys came with a message. "Hidalgo, you miserable dog, everyone is here. Sybaritic Samedis at Stetson's recommence. Till then. S."

I did not want to go. I well knew what attended me there. I had spent enough Saturday evenings (and many of the following Sundays) *chez* Stetson to last me a lifetime. But I did want to see Torquemada. I was curious to know what had become of him. I had reviewed our last conversation often during the time I was away. I had also lent him a not inconsiderable sum of money before departing and was hopeful that I might recover some of it. I decided to go to Stetson's, but only to see Torquemada.

The radiant and inconceivably wealthy Lucia Estrada was in attendance. Matanza, pomaded, unctuous, and solitary as always, was there. Vega, who had gone to India during the war in a vaguely ambassadorial capacity, greeted me cheerfully and introduced me to a delightful morsel of a woman to whom he gave the (fanciful?) sobriquet The Baroness. Morel, undersized and over-dressed, stood stiffly together with his retiring wife, Helena, in virtually the same spot I had last seen them occupy. Clara Larsen, even more excitable than she had been before the war, kissed me enthusiastically when I arrived; her taciturn husband, Javier, appeared shortly thereafter. Roderigo and Isabel Casanueva—surprisingly still affianced—giggled together in one corner with Castillo who regaled them, no doubt, with licentious stories of excess and intrigue at the palace. Matamoros and his handsome wife, Nicola, arrived just after

I did. Lady St. James, her feckless husband, Sebastian, and the others had promised to come later. There was no sign of Torquemada.

As before, the food was superb, the drink plentiful, the marijuana ubiquitous, smooth, and potent. Everyone behaved as if they had returned from summer vacations. "Europe," according to Matanza, "was boring." He swore never to go there again and we all laughed. Several people pretended interest in my American sojourn. I lied, telling them I had lectured at all the major universities; this seemed to satisfy their curiosity. Everyone expressed their relief and happiness to be back in Ixturria.

Conversation quickly focused on the small changes the war had engendered and the consequent difficulties these changes imposed on our little society. The *mulattas*, for example, had found employment in the factories during the war and were now unwilling to return to lower-paying domestic work. Everyone had finally hired blacks and Chinese to run their households. Lucia Estrada was still, after two weeks of searching, without a driver because she refused to entrust her Daimlers to anyone darker than a quadroon.

"We lost our mechanic," Morel said. "To the war. A casualty, it appears. The only one we know of."

The silence that followed was rescued from absurdity by Nicola Matamoros who asked, "What about a Chinese driver?"

"Yes," Lucia Estrada acknowledged, "I may be forced to find a Chinese driver. Do they drive?"

"Of course they do." Stetson said. Whether they are licensed is another matter."

"Oh, I don't give a damn about licences," Lucia Estrada answered, smiling.

"Did you drive here this evening then?" Nicola asked.

"*Jamais*," Lucia Estrada gave a dramatic shudder and we laughed.

"I picked her up," Matanza said.

"Driving is men's work," Lucia Estrada said, still smiling. Then, "Work is men's work." We all laughed again.

"Well," Roderigo said, "apart from difficulties with domestics, I am happy to report that very little appears to have changed in matters of consequence. I went to the Ministry of the Interior to see about my...export licence," there were chuckles at Roderigo's euphemism, "and was told that all exports, regardless of their nature, were now overseen, overseen and approved, that was the phrase she used—a stern young woman—exports were overseen and approved by a revolutionary committee at the Secretariat of Internal Development. Well, you can imagine my...."

"Blind panic," Clara suggested.

"My anxiety, shall we say," Roderigo resumed with a smile, nodding in Clara's direction. "I'm pleased to report that the compañeros at the Secretariat were eager to expedite my consignment. There were certain processing fees...."

"Naturally," Stetson said and we all laughed once again.

"*La plus ça change....*"

"Indeed."

The Matamoroses, who had been back longer than any of us and who shared an instinct for drama, had pieced together a tentative narrative of the war which explained why things appeared to have changed so very little. It was an exceedingly complicated tale featuring innumerable Byzantine alliances between political parties, opposing armies, and foreign powers and I lost interest less than halfway through. What had begun as a simple and fairly typical rebellion or revolution (depending on which newspaper you read and to whom you spoke) had mutated into a brutal and multifarious civil war because of internecine squabbling among the armed forces and ruptures among the rebels (or revolutionaries) along racial, religious, and ethnic lines. In typically Ixturrian fashion, no one had been able to agree with anyone else for long enough to accomplish anything significant and therefore, apart from a few cosmetic changes (and obviously a number of shot up buildings, bits of blasted countryside and a number—no one was really sure how many—of dead soldiers and rebels), nothing had been fundamentally altered.

"And where is Torquemada? What's happened to him?" I finally asked. Someone, perhaps Morel, said that he had heard Torquemada had been a collaborator. I laughed. It was such a ridiculous thing to say. The term was meaningless. Collaboration, as demonstrated by the story the Matamoroses had just told, was the *sine qua non* of political survival in Ixturria. I said as much but no one appeared to agree with me. No one knew anything about Torquemada though all agreed he had not left the country during the war and, therefore, was bound to make an appearance soon.

Clara's suggestion that I play them something on the piano was met with a general chorus of approval. Someone pressed a marijuana cigarette into my hand and I was led off in the direction of Stetson's shining Bösendorfer. I played a few short pieces: some Chopin and a sloppy Liszt, then an arpeggio-burdened improvisation. Clara gazed at me intently with her glittering eyes. I regarded her openly but did not smile. I wondered if her husband knew and realized suddenly I did not care at all if he did. I saw Nicola look at Clara and me but I pretended to be absorbed in my impromptu. It was the piano playing. Women, even in North America, have always mistakenly believed that my musical skills indicated turbulent and passionate currents running deep beneath my quiet exterior.

A popular saying in Ixturria claimed, "Sundays are rehearsals for death" and my first Sunday back was no exception. The weather was impossible and I was rendered exceedingly torpid by the combination of the humidity and the drugs I had consumed the night before. I felt as if I had regressed to where I'd been two years ago: perpetually bleary-eyed, somnolent, and entirely lacking in ambition. I lay on my bed and stared at the ceiling. Why had I come back here? To work, I told myself, but I knew that was a lie. I could work, if it was work I wanted, anywhere. Something else had drawn me back to Ixturria. A vortex of inertia perhaps.

The telephone rang. It was Clara. She was in the bar across the street and wanted me to join her. I told her I was resting. She said she'd come to see me then. Too tired to argue, I acquiesced, and told my gatekeeper to let her pass.

I offered her coffee, which she declined. I could tell from her feverish eyes that she had taken cocaine last night. She probably hadn't slept. She was anxious, brittle, and talked nonsense while fluttering restlessly around the room. I made few comments and struggled to keep my eyes open. She offered me some cocaine which I ungraciously accepted and inelegantly inhaled. Then, in an exaggeratedly theatrical manner, she kneeled beside my chair, put her head in my lap and confessed that she had missed me terribly. I said nothing. She kissed my hands and said she was "so very happy" that I had come back.

She looked up at me with concupiscence. I had to say something. I took her cold and small hands in mine while I searched my thoughts for something to tell her. I noticed the puckered needle marks in her forearms where she had injected herself. "Oh Clara," was all I could manage.

She offered to do certain things, and to allow me to do certain things to her that only the prostitutes of the shabbiest quarters permitted. "Don't talk like that," I said, but we made love in the darkened drawing room. She was thin, Clara, thinner than I remembered her, and restless, unsatisfied. After, I fell asleep. When I awoke she was gone.

I was very hungry but it was still too early to go out for dinner so I made coffee and smoked another low-grade cigarette—good cigarettes were only available on the black market and I had not yet found a houseboy to bring my weekly provisions. I wandered, naked, save for my dressing gown, smoking my stinking cigarette in the gloom of my darkened apartments. I might have felt disgusted with myself if I'd had more energy. As it was, I felt disappointed.

"Poor Clara." I said aloud. "Poor me. Poor, poor all of us."

Except perhaps Torquemada. He was the most likely one of us to have escaped the gravitational force of our clique. He had the most energy; he was the brightest, and the farthest-ranging, socially. I drank my coffee and recalled the conversation we had had before I left Ixturria. I had asked him if he thought he might leave later.

"Where would I go?" he had responded in a purely rhetorical tone. "Unlike the rest of you, I was born here. I am of this place."

"Are these the first faint stirrings of patriotism?"

"Worse, Hidalgo, worse." His hoarse laughter had attracted the attention of the other diners. I remembered several heads turned to regard him and that he had waved at them. And then, leaning over the table, in a conspiratorial voice he had said, "I believe in the revolution." He had laughed again when he saw my baffled expression.

"Very well," I had responded, gathering my wits, "but does the revolution believe in you?"

"We'll see. We'll see."

I imagined Torquemada tucked away in a camp in the sierras, organizing the resistance, inspiring the cadres, and invoking the spirit of the *Libertador* himself. I laughed for the first time since I'd landed in Ixturria. I resolved to find him.

Stetson's hedonistic soirées—which I attended in the hope of learning something reliable about Torquemada—almost attained their pre–war level of immoderacy. Our evenings swelled to include: numerous courtesans and paramours; lugubrious and insalubrious peddlers of fine opiates and narcotics; entertainments, including but not limited to: contortionists, eaters of glass, magicians, a bearded woman, and once, two spectacularly black and muscular men who thrilled us all with a bloody demonstration of the pugilistic arts. I played piano between rounds.

My inquiries regarding Torquemada were met with expressions of vague thoughtfulness or puzzlement. Morel said he'd been round to his place and it looked like it had been closed up for months. Gibson, an apocryphal character rumoured to be a pornographer, said he'd heard that Torquemada had left the city for the coast during the height of the war. The indifferent consensus seemed to be that Torquemada was enjoying the last few weeks of summer on the coast and would appear in the capital once the weather cooled.

I tried, unsuccessfully, to avoid Clara but she was tenacious. I consoled myself with the thought that I was able to exert a moderating influence on her. While with me, she stopped taking cocaine intravenously and confined her intoxicants to gin, served cold and in large quantities. I found myself lying about our *affaire* to many people but I did not believe I fooled anyone. My conscience did not bother me so much as the irritation and fatigue which Clara caused me. She had become tiresome and a burden.

I decided finally to go to Nuevo Plimoz, on the coast, to see if I could find Torquemada there. I had spent an idyllic month there several years ago, swimming, sleeping in the afternoons, drinking from his excellent wine cellar, eating splendid meals (I remembered, in particular, a wild suckling pig, and a marvellous tuna), and admiring the profusion of mimosas, dahlias, frangipani, magnolias, and other flowers that grew unattended in his gardens.

The journey, four hours by lazily puffing train, was pleasant enough, though much of the countryside I travelled through had been despoiled by the war. I ate a very good and rather large lunch with an excellent French Bordeaux. My post–prandial stupor evolved into an agreeable and dreamless siesta, and when I awoke I could smell the tart air of the green and hissing sea.

The sun beat down on me when I stepped off the train and I immediately hired a car to take me to Torquemada's place. I was very eager to see him, and indulged various daydreams where I stayed on with him, in quiet seclusion, enjoying a period of profound study and productivity, leaving behind the tedium of life in the capital. Torquemada's house, immense, off-white save for the red-tiled roof, and dating from the first days of the colonial period, soon became visible, perched, as it was, on the bluff, and staring blankly out to sea.

No one met the car at the gate, and we drove directly to the main house. The place did not seem to be abandoned but neither was there any immediate or obvious sign of human habitation. I wasn't entirely surprised by the situation. Torquemada was—and this may have been one of the strongest reasons for my feelings of affinity with him—the least wealthy member of our group. Land-rich, but cash-poor, he rarely maintained a permanent staff at any of his homes. He claimed he liked the solitude. It became evident that the main house was in use; I could see opened shutters and windows toward the rear of the building.

I walked along the side of the house, trying to keep to the stone path, now overgrown with weeds and grass. I rounded the quoin that gave on to the small courtyard partially roofed and shaded by eucalyptus trees, and heard a shrill whistle. Torquemada's melancholy and dusty parrot, Fulgencio, shifted from leg to leg on his perch. "Hello, you old lizard," I said. The beast beat his ragged and useless wings in response.

I stepped in the open door. The house was pleasantly cool and utterly quiet. I called hello but received no answer. I thought I'd find Torquemada in his study. I left my bag just inside the doorway and made my way down the dark, creaking hall. Only a few steps in, I heard Torquemada call, "*Quien es?*" When I didn't answer, he roared, "*Quien es?*" again, and then charged into the hallway from an adjoining room. He halted abruptly only a few paces in front of me.

His aggressive attitude and imposing size—I had forgotten just how large he was—startled me. "Torquemada, it's me. Hidalgo." I smiled and extended my hand.

"Hidalgo." He stood in the hallway, unmoving, and squinting at me. Then he drew himself out of his aggressive crouch to his full imposing height, stepped forward and smiled. "Hidalgo." He took my hand in his enormous one and shook it twice, very firmly. "Come, come, sit, sit." He indicated a small sitting room down the hall. "Why are you here?"

"I came to look for you," I said, as I lowered myself into a comfortable leather chair.

Hidalgo stood over me. "I thought you'd left." His tone betrayed some doubt.

"Well, I came back. As soon as the war was over."

"What a surprise," he said, but his voice was flat and lacking in enthusiasm. He nodded his tremendous square head, thinking, then clapped his hands together and asked, "A drink perhaps?" He disappeared for several moments then returned with two glasses containing a turbid, viscous liquid which I assumed to be a local *aguardiente*.

"Have you gone native, Torquemada?" I asked, raising my glass inquiringly. " I don't think I've ever tried this stuff. Is it as terrible as they say?

"Who says?"

I took a sip. It was rough, like ethyl alcohol tempered with sugar and cinnamon. "You're out of gin then?"

"What brings you here?"

"I told you. I came to look you up. No one seemed to know what had happened to you or where you'd gone so I thought I'd come have a look for myself." By way of reply, Torquemada offered only silence. "If my arrival is inopportune, tell me. There was no means of reaching you here. I am quite—"

He protested in demotic Spanish that he was simply surprised and insisted that I stay. Then he switched to English and said, perhaps by way of apology, "I've been alone here for some time. I'm very glad to see you." He raised his glass.

"How are you?"

"Fine," he said, I thought, rather equivocally. "And you? How are you? How have you been? Where have you been?"

"I'm well. I've been, you know, in America. My father has property there. It was interesting. I lectured in the universities, Ixturrian poetics, that sort of thing...." He nodded. "I've been back now just a little over a month and everything is at was. In all respects." I gave a low chuckle. "Except, of course, for your inexplicable absence." He said nothing so I continued. "You know, the bunch in the capital is as irritating as ever—"

"Why did you come back?"

"I don't belong in the United States. I knew no one there. The people there tolerated me because of my father, or they treated me as a curiosity." I surprised myself by continuing, "They are an appalling race, the Americans, loud, relentless, driven, ferocious in their appetite for something I'm sure they'll never find. They exhausted me. I don't belong there. I belong here."

"Do you?"

"Yes."

"Are you hungry?" he suddenly asked.

"No, I'm not, though if you have something to drink—other than that *aguardiente*—I wouldn't say no."

He went off to find some wine and while he was gone I prepared a marijuana cigarette. I was relieved that I could speak frankly to Torquemada. He returned with two bottles of Pouilly Fumé. "Will this do?"

"It will. It will do nicely." I held up the cigarette and asked—even though I'd never known him to smoke it, "Would you care for some of this?"

"No. Thank you."

He went to get some proper glasses and I lit my cigarette.

"Why do you smoke that?" he asked upon re-entering the room.

"I suppose I smoke it out of habit, to feel at ease. But I do try to use it sometimes to aid my thinking, to focus my thoughts on the essentials."

"The essentials?"

"Yes."

"Such as?"

"Certain metaphysical problems."

"Such as?"

"The meaning of life."

He erupted into laughter, the stentorian laughter I recalled. It was infectious, his laugh; I was soon sputtering and choking, and it sounded as if the parrot was moved to laughter as well. His raucous hoots echoed from the courtyard into the house. After Torquemada had calmed down, he asked me, "And what have you determined in your marijuana deliberations?"

"I haven't reached any conclusions yet."

"Smoke some more then."

"Indeed."

The familiar lustre was in his eyes. "You still dabble in the mystic arts then, Hidalgo? What's his name, The book of the something rose?"

"Hakim al-Madhi. The Book of the Secret Rose."

"Ah yes. How is it? Must be finished by now, no?"

"No. It is no closer to being finished than the last time you saw me. But I am confident, well, hopeful, that I will be able to undertake some serious work on it in the next few years. There was a degree of interest in the subject in certain circles in the United States."

We talked like this for some time, the wine and marijuana facilitating our conversation. "And what of your life these last years?" I finally asked.

He looked at me with a mixture of patience and incomprehension; it was a slightly condescending look but it was eventually superseded by his jumble-toothed smile. He shook his head and finished what was left in his glass. "My life?"

"Yes. How have things been? What did you get up to? Do you still believe in the revolution?"

"What about you? What do you believe in?" he asked, shifting his large frame in the ancient chair.

I had begun in an ironic mode but Torquemada was responding in tones of sincerity. I tried to deflect him. "Oh, I don't know. I think I'm a nihilist."

"I thought you were a mystic."

"An agnostic mystic nihilist perhaps."

Eventually, Torquemada produced bread, some cold meats, various ripe cheeses, and fruits, as well as two bottles of a hearty and drinkable domestic red wine. By nightfall, we were pleasantly inebriated.

"Morel, or Roderigo, or Matanza, one of that crowd in any case," I told him, "said you were a collaborator."

"Really." He plucked a grape from its stalk. "A collaborator."

"I said it was a rather meaningless term, in the context of Ixturria. Everyone is a collaborator here. There are no principled definitions of position here, only advantageous strategic alliances."

"Do you believe that?"

"Yes. I think so."

"Do you believe that everyone feels that way?"

"I imagine so."

"Really?"

"Well, I don't know. I have nothing to base that opinion on, you know." I admitted, "I don't actually know anyone other than, you know, that bunch, and my gatekeeper." I laughed.

"I don't think I've ever heard you say anything like that. I don't think I've ever heard you utter a statement that betrayed any awareness, or interest in the world," he paused here, searching, then settled on, "outside, at large."

"I'm aware of the world, you know, of politics, and so on. Politics, as someone aptly put it, is one of the forms of tedium. I'm not interested in that world. It, the world at large, the world out there," I flung my arm out, "is not particularly interested in me. So we get along quite well. Mutual indifference."

"And," he paused to regard me, "Do you imagine that things will always continue on in this way?"

"Well, yes. I don't foresee any cataclysmic changes. The war, for example, doesn't seem to have produced any lasting changes."

He looked at me intensely and I found his gaze disturbing. I looked back at him and said, in a slightly aggrieved voice, "What?" He looked away.

"Are you going to tell me about the war? All night, you've avoided the issue. You were the only one who stayed behind. What did you do? Did you organize a neighbourhood militia? Did you kill anyone?" I laughed rather stupidly. He turned his black eyes on me again and I immediately regretted my thoughtless remark.

He simply said, "The war's not over."

"I'm sorry?"

"It's not over, the war."

"It's not?"

"No."

"You mean there are still pockets of resistance in the..." I waved my hand, "sierras and...."

"Large pockets. But that is not what I mean. I mean that the Armed Forces plan to violate the cease-fire."

"What...? I'm not sure I understand." I corrected myself. "I'm sure I don't understand."

"The war is not over. This is a lull, a calm before the storm. The government plans a major offensive but before they have a chance to move, there will be a counter-offensive. Do you understand? It is about to start again."

I felt too addle-brained—the wine, marijuana, and lack of food—to grasp what he was telling me. I could not understand how he would know these things. I asked him about it.

"Who was it? Matanza, Roderigo? Said I was a collaborator? Not quite." He stood abruptly and closed a window. I heard him wander down the hall to close the door that opened onto the courtyard. Fulgencio hooted at him. An impression, an idea, was beginning to form in my mind but it seemed too improbable. There was, I was certain, a much simpler explanation.

Torquemada returned with a bottle of cognac and two snifters. He poured himself a glass. "You should go back to North America, Hidalgo," he said.

"I should go back."

"As soon as possible. And you should probably stay there."

"Because of the war that is about to break out, you mean."

He nodded, drank. Some moments passed. Then told me something incomprehensible. "My grandmother," he said, slowly, deliberately, "was a *mulatta*."

"Your grandmother."

"Was *mulatta*." He passed me a snifter of cognac.

"You...are...."

"An octoroon."

I stared at him. "I don't understand. I don't understand anything you've told me in the last ten minutes."

"I was an illegitimate child. My father had a quadroon mistress, my mother."

"How did you inherit? How.... Why didn't anyone notice?"

"I was brought up in my father's house because I was the only boy, his only son, but I was never allowed to forget—by my father or any member of his household or family—my low-born status. I was a strange hybrid of houseboy and only son. I learned to slide between worlds, to slip between houses, families, colours. I spent my entire life studying you and your kind; I am practically one of you. You never noticed because I never let you. I didn't want you to notice." There was silence and stillness in the house. Outside, the wind shifted the branches of the trees. "Do you understand what I'm saying?"

"No. I don't. I understand the words. I understand the words but I cannot accept, I cannot grasp the significance, the—" I gave up trying to express the thought. I felt as if everything, the green sitting room, the old house, the world itself, had in an instant, reversed itself, turned inside out. A certainty, at a fundamental level, had been shattered. I did not, like most of Ixturrian society, attach tremendous importance to racial distinctions; it was not the fact of Torquemada's miscegenation which disturbed me but, rather, something that felt like betrayal, his duplicity.

Smiling, he said, "You're surprised." I looked at him sharply and did not know what to say. He dropped his smile. "You're shocked, of course. I'm not the only one. In fact, there are a number of us, throughout Ixturrian society. Interlopers, impostors. We call ourselves Cuckoos, after the bird which lays—"

"Yes, I understand the reference."

"Don't take it personally, Hidalgo."

"No. I'm shocked. Well, I feel rather stupid. But it needn't change anything. It's not as if you've broken a law. It's just...I'm not sure. It is very unexpected." I finished my cognac. He quickly reached out his long arm and poured me some more.

"Everything will change, though, Hidalgo. This is what I'm trying to tell you. Ixturria as you know it is over, finished. There will be a war. In a very little while. Look." He left the room abruptly and I heard his footsteps in the hall. I drank my second cognac. I tried to make sense of my feelings but my meditations were interrupted by Torquemada's return. He held a leather portfolio which he passed to me.

"In there are copies of communiqués, directives, and memoranda regarding the offensive the government plans. Take a look." I let my hands float across the surface of the portfolio but did not open it. He continued, "In a few days, I will arrange to meet with several other Cuckoos and leaders of the revolutionary movements to prepare a co-ordinated response to the government's plans."

I sat there stupidly, staring at the worn leather of the case as if it might yield some answers. "I don't understand. How did you come to obtain these?" I tapped the portfolio.

"As a trusted advisor to the Minister of the Interior and my privileged status as a member of Ixturria's elite...well, anything is possible. Do you understand?"

"You've been a kind of spy."

"Yes. A kind of spy." His smile was not unkind. "It's very late."

"Is it? I should go then." I tried to raise myself from my chair. He laughed.

"I'm sure you don't intend to walk back down to the town now. You're more than welcome to stay here a few days. We have much to discuss. It's no trouble. I've already put your bag in the blue bedroom at the end of the hall off the stairs," he extended his arm, "to your right. You'll find everything you need there."

"Thank you."

"Oh." He shook his head: a gesture of modesty. "I like you Hidalgo. I don't know why exactly. You're shiftless but you're not harmful like some of the others. I trust that you'll take what I've told you to heart and make arrangements to leave the country as soon as possible."

"Yes, well. I can certainly see...I'll have to seriously consider it."

"Things here are finished, Hidalgo. This time, Ixturria will go up in flames."

"How apocalyptic."

"A purifying fire, perhaps. Then Phoenix-like, a new Ixturria will rise." He paused briefly, then said, "That's the idea at least." And he laughed, a laugh entirely free of bitterness.

The blue bedroom took its name from the wallpaper, a deep blue into which were set cream *fleur de lys*. The colour was soothing. The room was small but tastefully appointed. There was a washstand with a basin, an immense rosewood closet and a comfortable-looking bed, elaborately carved in an art nouveau manner. There was a leather chair and a small writing table.

I had brought the leather portfolio into the bedroom with me. I considered opening it and reading the documents within it but admitted to myself that I was not interested in the contents. I tossed the portfolio onto the table onto which I also placed my pants and shirt. I lay in the luxuriously soft bed and listened to the waves for a time and eventually fell into a heavy and slightly inebriated sleep. My dreams were jumbled, set simultaneously in Ixturria, the United States, and the Garden of the Secret Rose. The feeling of unseen forces massing on the fringes of my dreams became oppressive. At one point in the night, I thought I heard urgent voices and noises in the house and made an effort to wake out of my dream, but was unable to do so.

I woke with a cloudy head, but the hunger I felt cut through my stupor and urged me to get up to search for nourishment. The house was quiet and I had no idea if Torquemada was still sleeping or if he had begun his day's activities. I could find no bottled water in the kitchen. I assumed he must have more laid away somewhere but did not know where he kept such things and was not about to tramp all over the house in search of it. I hoped he would appear shortly and provide me with the necessities. I boiled water for coffee, of which there was plenty, and peeled an orange.

I drank the coffee and ate the orange, along with some hard but not unpleasant biscuits I had found. I recalled the previous evening's conversation but in the light of the clear morning it had taken on an unreal quality, and I entertained the optimistic possibility that Torquemada's bizarre disclosures had been little more than troubling dreams.

I decided, feeling somewhat clearer in my head, to venture down to the sea. The stony beach, arrayed in a patchwork of dark green seaweed, was utterly deserted save for a few birds, which wheeled far above my head, calling out in their forlorn voices to one another. I walked, shoes in hand, to the edge of the water. The ocean was flat and the colour of steel. I stood there for some time, lost in vague contemplation of the sea. I thought of the creatures that dwelt deep below its surface; of the continents that lay beyond it; of the ships that traversed it, and the aeroplanes that passed over it. I imagined crossing that sea again. I thought vaguely of Switzerland, but knew that since the last members of my mother's family had died I would find no welcome there. I did not want to return to the United States; I did not want to leave Ixturria.

Perhaps it would not be necessary. Perhaps I could find a place in the new Ixturria that Torquemada had prophesied. I was—he had said so himself—harmless. Perhaps the revolution would ignore me and allow me to live out the rest of my days in the solitary, quiet, and harmless contemplation of the metaphysical questions which intrigued me. I wanted to talk further with Torquemada and hoped he was now awake or, better still, returned from the market with supplies and food.

The house was quiet, except for Fulgencio's intermittent mutterings, odd clucks, and occasional whistles. There was no evidence that Torquemada was awake. I felt certain (a feeling in the air of the house) that he was still asleep and thought I might wake him by rummaging noisily in the library which was adjacent to the room in which he preferred to sleep. On approaching the library, I noticed the door to his room was ajar. I knocked on the door. There was no answer. I knocked again and, receiving no response, I pushed the door open.

Torquemada's great bulk lay twisted sideways across the bed, almost falling out of it, inert, but wearing a fixed and awful, open-mouthed expression on his face. His throat had been slit. His body and bed linen were covered in discoloured, dried blood. His room was in utter disarray. An involuntary and unrecognizable sound issued from deep within my guts. I stood transfixed in the doorway until terror impelled me to move. I ran, yelling and moaning inarticulately, through the house, unsure of what to do. Finally, I ran up the stairs to the blue bedroom, snatched up my belongings, and ran out of the house.

I ran like a deranged person. I ran, and fell halfway down the gravel road that led to the house, ripping my trouser leg at the knee and cutting my skin. I vomited unexpectedly. It was then I realized I had picked up the leather portfolio that Torquemada had shown me the night before. My mind was completely confused. I ran on, clutching my bag and Torquemada's portfolio, in the sinister shade of the cypresses, onto the main road, into the sunlight, into the town.

My dishevelled appearance and still agitated countenance elicited some disapproving commentary from the mid-day patrons of the Grand Hotel Bar. I ignored them, and ordered French, not national, cognac. It was all I could do to remain calm while the waiter brought it. I took it from his hands and stopped myself from immediately ordering another. I drank. The alcohol imposed a tenuous order on my thoughts.

I realized now that Torquemada's killer—or killers?—might not have been thieves. The terrifying occurrence may have had something to do with what he had told me last night: the Cuckoos and the impending conflict. My thoughts leapt to my own safety. Did whoever had killed Torquemada know I was there? What would happen if it were discovered that I had been there on the night of his death? Might I be held responsible in some way? And who was it that would hold me responsible? My thoughts reeled with the variables. I thought, not without a ridiculous sort of pity, of the parrot. I thought of the papers in my possession. I waved to the waiter to bring me another cognac, and inquired of him the time of the next train to the capital. He told me there was one leaving on the hour, in approximately thirty-three minutes. I thanked him, settled my bill, then walked to the train station.

I obtained a sleeper. I drew the curtain and changed my clothes. After changing, I went to the restaurant car, taking Torquemada's leather portfolio with me. I ate some food and soon felt more steady. I did not open the portfolio.

As the train approached the long bridge over the swiftly flowing Rio Victoria, I left the restaurant car and stood between it and the next car. I lowered the window on the door, waited till we were over the river, and threw the portfolio into the water. I closed the window and returned to my sleeper. I lay down on the bed. I lay there, without sleeping or moving, until we reached the central station.

I fearfully locked myself into my apartments for several days. I spoke to no one and did not go out. To keep calm I consumed quantities of laudanum and gin, but even so I slept very poorly and ate next to nothing. I jumped at every small noise. I imagined, at the very least, that the police would come around to ask questions. I tried, at first, to turn my thoughts away from the memory and image of Torquemada's death, but, later, as it became apparent that news of the event had not reached the capital, I held onto the image of Torquemada's enormous corpse sprawled across the bed, in an effort to investigate its details and diminish the power it held in my imagination.

At Stetson's Samedi, Lucia Estrada greeted me with one of her radiant smiles. I spoke cheerfully with her for some time, ignoring Clara's woeful looks. Later, I took a large quantity of marijuana, and spent the remainder of the evening at the piano. Bent over the glittering keyboard, I resolved to imitate the example of my friends gathered at Stetson's that night. If I could, as they had, forget Torquemada entirely, or at least consign him to a remote corner of my memory, then nothing would come of the recent disagreeable episode. No police inquiry and no armed conflict would challenge my benign presence in Ixturrian society. Forgetting Torquemada in this way was not, I realized, disrespectful or a sign of moral cowardice, but rather, a magical act that would align my will with the universal, insulate my life more perfectly, and allow me to realize my hitherto unconscious destiny of becoming Lucia Estrada's husband.